THUNDER FROM A CLEAR BLUE SKY

a novel

Justin Bryant

ISBN: 979-8-9874654-1-7

Cover design by Angelo Maneage
Airplane photo by Pavol Svantner on Unsplash

Published January 2023 by Malarkey Books

malarkeybooks.com

For Sarah

ON THE FLIGHT DECK of a 1941 production DC-3, first officer Oscar Labruna, studying the radar, sees that there is a line of storms across Panama and extending into the Mosquito Gulf. The storms have been routing commercial air traffic far out to sea, but Labruna knows he will not have the luxury of diverting; they don't carry enough fuel for such a detour. Labruna can't yet tell from his radar where the strongest storms are waiting, but he's not nervous; he enjoys the challenge presented by bad weather. "I don't fly the plane," he likes to brag. "I orchestrate it."

The pattern of the storms begins to appear on his radar. The plane is over seventy years old, but it has been retrofitted with the latest and best avionics and engines. Labruna is surprised and a little concerned by what he sees. He can switch views to examine the storm by rainfall amount and temperature, and can view lightning strikes superimposed over both. There is not much rain, and the frequency of lightning is only moderate, but the clouds appear light blue. They are cool. This is because they are towering high into the stratosphere, far above the plane's maximum altitude.

Labruna looks forward, out the cockpit windows. There is nothing to see but black sky and wispy vapor illuminated by their running lights. It is 9:14 p.m. He looks at Captain Ferrera, seated to his right.

"It's going to be bumpy," Labruna says.

"I can see that," Ferrera replies, leaning over to check the radar himself.

"It's not my favorite thing, junking around at night in weather when you can't see a damn thing," Ferrera says. Then he laughs, and wipes a hand across his mouth.

Labruna tunes to Panama City radio for local weather. It is clear, light wind, at the airport, but that is still two hundred miles away, and somewhere in between them are mountains of boiling cloud. His radar indicates they are approaching the edge of the first storm, but ahead in the dark night they still see nothing. Labruna cranes his head upward and sees a few stars. This reassures him, for now.

"My aircraft," Ferrera says. He has been in control of the flight throughout, but this is his way of reminding Labruna not to input the flight controls.

"I suppose I'd better tell him," Ferrera says, almost to himself. He picks up the intercom, pauses for a moment, and asks their passenger to come to the cockpit.

The man enters. He is tall and strongly built, with thick forearms and fingers and muscles on his back and neck that spread his shirt collar wide. Ferrera explains the problem with the storm. The tall man listens, but Labruna can tell he's not really hearing. He's got something else on his mind. Ferrera suggests the man strap himself into his jump seat. The tall man exits, and Labruna and Ferrera turn back to the problem of the storm.

Labruna's radar is now a mosaic of green, yellow, and red pixels. They are close enough that he can begin to discern the structure of the storm system. It's both good and bad news: it is a highly powerful multi-cell cluster, but there appear to be gaps and valleys between the cells. Already his mind makes sense of the colors and patterns. He can see a route through.

"Here we go," he says. He smiles quickly at Ferrera. "Left, two-two-zero. That's good. Hold that."

Ahead of them, suddenly, faintly illuminated, is the storm. The cloud structures provide reference for their speed. They are hurtling towardthe gray-black mountains, but the valley he'd seen on radar is there. "Left, left, just a little," he says. Ferrera eases them between the cells.

"A little buffeting," Ferrera says, referring to feedback in his stick, but the air is still smooth.

"Okay, it'll—you can level, and then we'll have to turn hard right. You can see it, there. Turn. Turn."

Ferrera banks them to the right. The right wingtip is clear of the storm cell by less than a hundred feet. Out his window on the left side, Labruna looks up for the stars, but sees only the neighboring cell looming above them. He scans the radar. The valley is closing fast. The cells are colliding around them. They are at twenty-five thousand feet, their maximum altitude.

"Right, um, there's still a gap, but it's closing. You'll level here and then right at two-two-six, and then...it may close on us, but it's narrow there. We'll be through it in fifteen seconds."

"Out the other side?" Ferrera asks.

"Yeah," Labruna answers uncertainly. But looking at the radar, he already knows he's wrong. Out the windows, he sees the valley coming to a dead end, and the wall of cloud, primed with moisture and driven higher by updrafts at the front of the squall line, now rising impossibly above them. There is nowhere to turn.

Before Labruna can say anything, Ferrera sees it too, and mutters, "Shit."

"Can we jump it?"

"We can try," the captain answers.

Ferrera nudges the throttle and eases the nose slightly up. The plane responds initially, but Labruna knows this is dangerous. If the plane isn't able to climb any further, the nose-up attitude will cause them to lose airspeed and, quickly, altitude.

"Twenty-five three," Labruna says, reading the altimeter. They've climbed three hundred feet.

"We need more."

Labruna no longer feels exhilarated by the challenge. Adrenalin has been replaced by dread. Solid cloud walls are all around them now. It's like slaloming through skyscrapers a hundred feet above city streets. Lightning explodes right outside their windows. He has been listening to commercial flights chatter about the storm on the radio. He would like to join in, ask for route suggestions or just for best wishes, but, of course, he can't. The tall man pays them to be invisible.

Graveyards in the sky. That's what his first flight instructor used to call thunderstorms. The cloud wall rushes up to meet them.

"She's strong," he says to Ferrera, but really to reassure himself. "She can take anything." They look at each other and force smiles.

Cloud swallows them. For two or three seconds the air remains smooth, and then there is a single *bang*! and they are jolted upward with a floating sensation, the kind you get when you hit a pothole too fast on a country road. Labruna can feel the plane settling back into its trajectory, and then the turbulence comes. It throws the plane as if it is in the jaws of a giant terrier, up and down, left and right. A downdraft hits the right wing and snaps them into a forty-degree bank. Ferrera struggles to level. There follows a series of smaller but incredibly violent bumps, blurring the instruments to the point where Labruna can't read the altimeter or airspeed indicator. The plane sounds like nickels shaken in a tin can, all groaning metal, slaps and bangs, deeper thudding from the cargo hold. He thinks of the old joke about DC-3s: a collection of loose parts flying in tight formation. It doesn't seem funny now.

Incandescent white light explodes in front of them, filling the windows and cockpit. Labruna is momentarily blinded. The sound is unexpectedly muted, a muffled, metallic groan, and all the instrument panels and interior lights blink off. The cockpit is dead. Labruna's eyes adjust rapidly; without any glare or interior illumination, the clouds outside swirl in a mix of charcoal, black, and white.

"Lightning strike," Ferrera says. "Engines?" he asks.

Without instrumentation, Labruna cannot be sure, but his instincts, and the way his body feels in his seat, tell him that they are still being propelled forward.

"Engine one good," he says. "Engine two...good."

Labruna begins the process of rebooting the interior power. When he flips the final switch, there is a reassuring click and a flicker of light. Before power returns completely, he looks out the window again, and something to his left catches his eye. They are still plowing through heavy cloud, but through it he sees the silhouette of a plane flying abreast but above him by several hundred feet, backlit by more flashes of lightning.

"Proximity warning," he says, almost in disbelief.

"What?"

"Proximity warning, ten o'clock. They're above us."

Ferrera begins turning them to the right just as cockpit power returns in a series of blinking lights. Labruna checks both his radar and Airborne Collision Avoidance System screen, but the first is blank, and the second is still booting up. He sees the plane again, receding as they turn away. It is a DC-3 of the same vintage as theirs.

"There," he says, pointing. Ferrera looks over and sees it.

The plane disappears into cloud.

"What the hell," Ferrera says, angry and mystified. "Does he have another plane up here with us?"

Another series of violent jolts rocks the plane. Labruna scans his radar for any sign of relief, and then— "There might be a gap opening at your two o'clock."

"I see it!" Ferrera has continued the climb, helped by strong updrafts, and they are nearly out of the top of the storm. For a split second they find clear air, and he banks towarda seam between cells. But it closes just as fast, and again they crash and bang against masses of moisture-heavy cloud. At one point, a downdraft drops them three hundred feet in three seconds. Ferrera fights it and slowly begins to climb again. Labruna looks up. Solid cloud gives way in places to gauzy haze. Patches of black sky begin to show.

"Climb, climb," he urges quietly. He sees a single star shining through the haze. They burst through a final curtain of mist, and suddenly they are skimming along the top of the storm. His radar goes black. The sky ahead and above them is awash in stars. They are free. The plane flies smooth and true.

Ferrera sighs and says simply, "Fuck."

Labruna peers over his shoulder and can see part of the gray wall of the storm receding, still spitting lightning. The Captain descends to twenty-three thousand feet. He leans back in his seat and stretches his neck.

Labruna, his fingers trembling, reduces the gain on the radar so he can see the storm again, already five miles behind them. Although it is long and winding like a serpent, there is a bulge in the center, where multiple cells are colliding, and he can see that it is tracking to the west, towardthe Gulf of Chiriquí. It will either spend its venom there, or continue to grow into something that makes the news.

The tall man comes back into the cockpit. He still looks fierce, but Labruna thinks he looks a little shaken, too.

"Are you okay, sir?" Ferrera asks.

The tall man doesn't answer. He is coiled and tense, like the storm itself. Labruna can see his rib cage expand with each breath. The tall man looks past them, out the cockpit windows. A carpet of benign cloud glides below, faintly illuminated by the tapestry of stars above, and a sliver of moon, newly risen. His breathing slows.

"It's beautiful," he says.

The clouds unroll beneath them. The engines hum and the radio crackles with chatter, pilots and air traffic control trying to fight the storm, but to Labruna it feels very quiet in the cockpit.

"Yes," Ferrera agrees. "Yes, it's beautiful."

"You must see beautiful things all the time from up here."

Ferrera looks at Labruna. "Yes sir, we do."

The tall man crosses his arms in front of his chest as he stares out the cockpit windows. "I envy you," he says. "I took flying lessons when I was a teenager. Single-engine plane. But other things got in the way."

Labruna wonders if the man has any idea how dangerous the storm was.

"Maybe this is heaven," the tall man says. "To fly forever on a beautiful night, and never have to land?"

"Who can say, sir," Ferrera answers.

"What a Heaven that would be," the tall man says. "To never land. To stay up here, with the moon." He shakes his head. "Well, right. Who can say? Who can really say?"

He nods again, then returns to the cabin.

Captain Ferrera exhales deeply.

Labruna looks out the window to his left, but sees only the receding storm.

***

Geoff had torn himself from his comfortable life like weeds ripped by the roots from wet earth, and wasn't even sure why he'd done it. He had chosen instead a life of walking, through jungle and over plains and across desiccated citrus groves, where the fruit grew as dry and stringy as old rope, and alongside rushing rivers hiding crocodiles and snakes and huge fish with iridescent scales. He had chosen exhaustion, nights of numb stupor while resting in derelict United Fruit Company boathouses with his squadron, leaning together in silence like depleted magnets in an abandoned power station. They had as companions clouds of mosquitoes and ripping hunger, fever dreams and waking nightmares, but also enough beauty to swell the oceans of the heart: distant storms stabbing lightning into limestone hills, moonrises over untended fields, galaxies of lightning bugs illuminating plains of wild mountain grass.

They had, at last, one great blessing: a tremendous weariness that followed them like a faithful dog, step by step, so that death, if it came, would not be entirely unwelcome.

It had all been a mistake.

In the long weeks and months that had now stretched over four years in The Free State, Geoff had often reflected on the moment of his terrible decision, and the source of all his regret. It was the day they saw the dog on a visit to the Maryborne Sunday Market. A local animal shelter was holding an adoption day, and a pit bull puppy, just a baby, followed them with glossy eyes as they walked around looking at the dogs in their crates.

"You like him, don't you?" Geoff asked.

"He's so sweet," Elena said. "Look how he keeps looking at us."

The little dog cocked its head to one side, its floppy ears hanging past its jowls.

"I can take him out for you, if you want to play with him," a young woman volunteer said.

Elena looked at Geoff, expectant.

"Why not, if you want to," he said.

The woman brought them inside a small fenced area, then led the little puppy inside. She released his leash, and he bounded over to Elena and pressed himself into her body as she laughed in delight.

"He's so beautiful! What's his name?"

"This is Snacks," the woman said.

"Snacks!" Elena repeated. "Well, you're a beautiful boy, Snacks!"

Geoff reached out a hand and stroked the dog's neck. It twisted its head back to look at him.

"What do you think?" the volunteer asked. "Do you want to apply for him?"

Elena looked at Geoff. He laughed. "Are you sure you're ready to walk him, to pick up after him, train him?"

"We'll get him together," she said. "He'll be ours."

"But I'm taking the position," he said. "With The Free State."

There it was. The words were out. His stomach felt frozen, as if he'd gulped a pint of icy sludge. He hadn't even made up his mind yet, or so he'd thought. He'd been debating taking the position with The Free State for weeks in his mind, and had only once mentioned it to Elena, as an offhand possibility.

She flinched, but only for a moment. The dog pawed playfully at her face. She scrunched up her nose and kissed him on his tiny forehead.

"I was going to tell you at the right time," he added.

"I didn't know it was a serious possibility."

"They do a savings match for university, so I can go without a loan in a couple of years."

She scratched the puppy under his chin; the dog leaned his head back and yawned. The volunteer, noticing the tension, had begun moving away, but Elena called her back.

"Bring me the application, please," she said.

He'd replayed that conversation a hundred times, a thousand. There he was, at home with Elena, any number of possible futures ahead of him, and now...well, now he was in the rainforest, not quite starving but always hungry, always exhausted but incapable of real sleep, not a real soldier and not fighting a real war, but not safe, either.

"Stop," Logan said softly from ahead. His metal detector had begun to blink. He swung it side to side, identified the mine, and waved Geoff and the others around it. The sun came through stagnant clouds and covered the squadron as they crossed an open patch of jungle. These clearings were sometimes mined, left over from forgotten conflicts or training exercises. Three-legged dogs were common in the jungle provinces.

Geoff didn't think of Elena and Snacks or his regrets when it was quiet or when he was bored, which had become almost a default state. He could control his thoughts at those times. It was during increasingly rare moments of danger, as now, inching through a minefield, that he found himself remembering the back of Elena's legs or the arch of her eyebrows or her pleasing candy smell—perfume she bought on trips to Wilshire mixed with the sweet soap she used to scrub her farm body. He thought of her carefree laugh and, in contrast, her work-toughened hands. His memories of her were so vivid, and his longing so great, that times came when he could not help but cry out in frustration, a miserable sort of howl that he disguised by holding his head and feigning a migraine.

He had seen Elena only a half-dozen times since he joined, on short leaves and one nine-day extended break. For a time, they had both expected to pick up where they left off, when The Free State operation finally ended. Now, when together or by email, they never spoke of the future.

They crossed the clearing and trooped back into the darkness under the canopy. The shade brought relief from the heat, but at the cost of heavy undergrowth which made every step a labor. Sawgrass tore at their hands and clouds of mosquitoes plagued them, until they finally stopped.

"This is what life's all about," Six said. "Good friends enjoying a fun walk on a beautiful day. What more could you want? And to think we get paid for this!"

Geoff and Logan laughed. They had not been paid for months. Emma, a mine sweeper like Logan, pushed past them. "Out of the way, Six," she said. "Working people coming through."

Joshua, their squad leader, spread them out in a semicircle facing an animal trail that led to a stream. Geoff settled his weapon on his shoulder and folded himself into the greenery. He kept his eyes on the animal trail. It was already starting to grow over; there were no more big animals in the forests. Hungry Free Staters had shot and eaten them all.

His stomach spasmed with hunger. Above them, a small spotter plane buzzed over the jungle canopy. He could see a depression in the undergrowth thirty meters to his right, where Logan had settled into the ferns. Logan had once mentioned leaving a girlfriend behind. That wasn't the kind of thing they talked about often, but Geoff had not forgotten it.

He rubbed his eyes and massaged his temples, trying to disengage the headache that had recently begun to trouble him, a product of chronic dehydration and sleep deprivation. They had plenty of time to sleep, but his was marred by insects, rain, and, lately, dreams. He kept his eyes on the trail and shook off his thoughts of Elena, saved for later his fantasies and his fears of reunion.

They found no game, not even a jungle rat, and went to sleep hungry. He let Elena come to him, then, and she talked him through his hunger and pain, until he fell into something almost like sleep.

***

Geoff, plagued by headache, lay curled in his damp hole in the ground, beginning to dream while still awake. A white mist rose from the ferns and covered him; his eyelids drooped, his world went white, and then he was on a plane, a commercial jet, seated next to a window. He had never flown before, and the view of the earth sliding thirty thousand feet below astonished him. He turned to the man seated next to him—the only other passenger on the plane—but he was reading a magazine, and Geoff could tell he didn't want to be bothered.

Something caught his eye, on the edge of his field of vision, ahead of the plane; a kind of shadow or darkness. He pressed his left cheek against the window, but still couldn't quite see what was ahead.

"I wouldn't worry about it," his neighbor said.

Geoff turned to look at him. The man put the magazine facedown on his lap, keeping his spot in the pages.

"It looks like a storm," Geoff said.

"I wouldn't worry about it," the man repeated. He smiled and picked the magazine back up.

He hadn't been worried about it, or at least he didn't think so. But now he was. He pressed his face flat against the window again. Yes. Yes, it was definitely dark up ahead.

"The pilot will fly around it," Geoff said, as much to himself as to the man. He looked at the man from the corner of his eye.

"Let's just put our faith in the pilot," the man said, with a small laugh.

Geoff caught the faintest whiff of smoke. Looking back out the window, he thought they were getting closer; the sliver of dark at the edge of his window seemed to grow. He looked down at the earth, and though what he saw was just an indistinct jumble of fields and lakes and streets, he knew it was something else: home.

"Can we land here?" he said. "This is where I'm going."

"Ah. No," the man said, leaning over to look out the window. He appeared incapable of blinking. "You know better than that. You're not ready."

Geoff started to protest, to point out the window. "You'll be fine," the man said, the hard lines of his face softening. "Don't you remember? We do this all the time."

"We?"

"You and I," the man said. "Every night."

He wore a charcoal gray suit with a white shirt and black tie. Atop his short, severe haircut rested a pair of aviator sunglasses. Fine lines spread around his eyes and the corners of his mouth. His skin had a faint glittery tint to it and looked textured, as if he were coated in powdered diamonds.

Around the man, everything suddenly fell in on itself: the plane turned to cloud, his seat fell away beneath him, the ground rushed up to meet him, and then the jungle, and the men sleeping in their holes. He was back in his. The man in the suit was gone, but he heard his voice: "All things converging." And he remembered now that this is what always happened when he slept: night after night, with this man in the gray suit, this shark man, he was annihilated in the sky.

***

It's *Time to Stand Up for Your Country*

Freedom. Liberty. Peace. Prosperity. Values Calem was founded upon when we gained formal independence from Great Britain in 1955. Now those values are threatened by The Dirt Tigers, radical, violent anarcho-Communists who want to appropriate your family's farmland or the corner store your grandfather built with his own hands, and turn public parks and playgrounds into indoctrination centers. This is where YOU come in. Join The Free State. Men and Women who join will receive a government salary in addition to tuition matching for university, health care, and, best of all, any and all outstanding student loan payments will be suspended for the duration of your term of service. You may even be eligible to have some portion of your loans permanently canceled!***

Stop by your local recruitment office today. Do it for your family. Do it for yourself. Do it for your country. The Free State. To Preserve the Calem Way of life.

**interest will continue to accrue*

***up to eighteen percent of outstanding balances*

***

Hi Geoff,

I've started looking for an apartment in the city. Not to move, not permanently at least, but just to spend a few days there a week. I haven't told my father. It's going to have to stay a secret. I already sleep on Trin's couch a couple nights a week, but that's no good, because a) she's out in Linerville, which isn't really even the city, and b) her boyfriend stays over sometimes, and I feel like I'm in the way, even though they say I'm not.

I look every day online. Somewhere near Hilltop or anything south of the river, really, where you can walk everywhere, there are parks and shops and markets and a couple of movie theaters. A lot of street vendors, too. I want to see people, to be able to go listen to music, be able to wake in the morning and walk someplace close for good coffee and a biscuit. That kind of thing.

I'm looking at places between c1200-1400 a month. You can't get much for that. Just a studio, probably no elevator, no outside space, but I can just about afford it. I won't have much money for anything else, but it will be worth it. I want to be able to walk in Pullman Park, and watch the dogs play on the hill, and not have to worry about what time the bus leaves to go back to the farm. I really think the city is where I'm meant to be. Every day, I hope dad agrees to sell the farm and retire. Then I can make the move full time. And he can learn to relax.

Wilshire has changed a lot since you've been gone. Rent has really skyrocketed. Maybe you'd like it, especially after all this time in the jungle. I see older women walking with their shopping, and I think how great that must be, to walk everywhere, to carry your shopping home each day. To me, anyway, that's a wonderful kind of life.

Stay safe,

Elena

***

Geoff had an itch on the back of his neck. He shifted his rifle to his left hand and rubbed at it with his right, then flicked the sweat from his fingertips. He had been crouching in heavy bush next to a hardwood tree for three hours. There was an animal trail nearby, leading to a stream. The squad could supplement their meager rations tonight if he shot a deer or spider monkey, but the best he realistically hoped for was a tree rat.

As darkness began stealing under the canopy, he heard, or rather felt, something approaching. He saw the silhouettes at fifty meters. Four people—no, five—moving with casual ease. Two women and three men. He backed deeper into the bush until he found Logan. They sat in silence, hidden in ferns, as the figures came down the trail. Livingston was hidden another hundred meters along; the rest of the squad equally spaced. It wouldn't do to have them surprised.

Geoff whistled twice; the figures stopped.

"We're ahead of you," Geoff said.

"How many?" a voice returned.

"Two of us here. Eight more ahead. All in cover."

"You're still hunting for your dinner?" the voice asked.

"You know how it is."

"Come out, mate. We have food for you."

Geoff looked at Logan.

"Don't be proud," the voice said. "Everyone deserves to eat."

"You know we're not supposed to," Logan said.

"We understand the need to maintain appearances," a woman's voice said. "We'll leave it right here. Take it. We'll leave more for the others ahead."

Geoff and Logan didn't respond.

"Don't forget you're only out here because your government lied to you."

They waited until the Dirt Tigers had moved down the trail, then emerged from the ferns to find two sealed, military-issue MREs—meals ready to eat. They also left a can of insect repellent and a package of waterproof matches.

"You want the pork or chicken?" Geoff asked.

"Pork."

Later, despite their hunger, they forced themselves to eat slowly.

"Have you ever considered," Six said, "that we're the bad guys here? Like, if this was a movie. We're the powerful force sent to repress—"

Logan paused mid-bite. "We're not powerful," he said softly. "They're feeding us."

"It doesn't matter," Geoff said. "It doesn't matter who's good and who's bad. We signed up. We're here."

"But what if we're bad," Six said. "That's all I'm saying."

They finished eating, then sat talking late into the night, knowing there wasn't particularly much to do tomorrow.

***

The insect repellent left by The Dirt Tigers had an artificial citrus scent. As soon as it hit Geoff's nose, it swept him back to the small stand of fruit trees with Elena on the

Telford farm, the one spot where Mr. Telford couldn't see them even when he was in his fields. They would climb the trees and he would try to make her laugh. He sometimes ate an entire lemon—bitter peel, seeds, and all—to impress her. She only howled in protest. He did pull ups from branches. She would smile and try to get butterflies or ladybugs to land on her fingers. If that didn't work, she would hunt up a modest-sized tarantula and let it crawl on the back of her hand. They were fourteen years old.

That, at least, was how he now remembered it, but part of him knew it could not have always been that good.

He would run home after dark and lie awake in bed with his hands behind his head and wonder why it was that he wanted to kiss her, and what it would be like if he did. She tried to talk to him about things, serious things, but he was usually forced to pretend to understand or blindly agree, which she saw through. He lived every day with a curious pressure in his chest—not unpleasant—that only went away when he wasn't thinking of her.

The arrow of time moves in only one direction. He couldn't stay in the past, much as he wanted to. The arrow brought him back.

"I hope they come back tomorrow," Logan said, after the other men had bunked for the night. "I could get used to food again."

Geoff raised the mosquito repellent and sprayed a small amount into the air, closed his eyes and leaned into the misty cloud, and again defied the arrow of time.

***

Geoff woke to tiny red fires like candles moving through the trees. The others slept. He lifted his head and rested on his elbows. The red flames, in a small cluster, moved toward him, paused, then moved again, with a slight bobbing motion. He rose slowly and began to reach for his rifle, but was overcome with an abiding sense of peace, and so left it lying in his sleep hole. The red flames moved again, and a shape stepped into the clearing thirty feet in front of him.

It looked like a deer, a large buck, but with a paisley pattern to its coat and candle flames atop each point of its variegated antlers. It gazed directly at him, passive and calm. Geoff could hear its steady breathing. He glanced over his shoulder, but the others still slept. He was asleep too, he decided. The red flames danced in time with his own beating heart. The deer took another step toward him.

"All things converging," it said flatly, though its mouth did not move.

After a few moments it turned and walked back into the forest, tiny flames flickering through the growth like newborn lightning. Geoff didn't remember these details when he woke in the morning, only the most nebulous sense of having been visited, but he went through the day feeling protected somehow. Loved, even.

***

"Listen," Six said. "I know this town, Haslemere, south of the cane fields. There's a veterans hall there. If we—"

"What do you mean, 'the cane fields'?"

"You know. Sugar cane."

"There are a million sugar cane fields all over the place. Which ones do you mean?"

"The ones near Haslemere. What I was saying was, if we end up moving that way, we could go to the veterans hall and they'd give us a decent meal."

Geoff wiped his forehead with the back of his hand. "A veterans hall isn't going to give a meal to deserters," he said.

"I'm not talking about deserting. I mean we can all go together."

"You're always talking about deserting."

"That's a dramatic way of putting it. I just want to go home. Because unlike you, I can admit we all fucked up by coming out here in the first place."

Geoff covered the fire with damp soil. It smoldered and kept the mosquitoes at bay.

He crossed his rifle in front of his chest and stared up into the trees. Clouds had gathered earlier, building with the heat. Rain was coming.

"There are probably women there, too," Six said. "In Haslemere."

Geoff smiled. "Sure there are."

He had deleted most of Elena's emails eventually. He felt it wasn't entirely healthy to keep rereading them, looking for clues or context between the lines, even when she wasn't remotely ambiguous. In the early days, when they passed near a town, or an isolated tower, their phones would begin buzzing with notifications, and everyone would stop to read their texts and emails. Sometimes, he'd have enough of a signal to receive messages, but his attempts to reply would often die in the outbox, the progress bar stuck on a random number like 43%. Increasingly, with almost nowhere to charge their phones, they were largely cut off from the outside world. He had saved a few of the emails, though.

You'll be back one day and we'll see what happens then.

"In Haslemere, Haslemere, my baby's got a new dress," Six sang softly from his hole. Geoff rolled on his side and forbade his mind from wandering, but it didn't work. He knew the rich students whistled at Elena when she went to the city. He didn't worry about them; she didn't like braggarts and flirts. It was the quiet ones, the ones he had seen himself, with funny glasses and clothes that didn't quite fit, that he worried she might notice. She liked outsiders. He knew she must be lonely. Who was he to begrudge her company? Nobody chooses to be lonely for long if they have options.

"In Haslemere, Haslemere..." A breeze came and Six's voice fell away in it. His head dropped. Then he snapped back awake. "One day, all this will be over," he said. "And we'll laugh about how we used to sleep in mud."

Soon it began to rain.

***

This is Sister Susie with Dirt Tiger Radio, broadcasting from the jasmine-scented mountains of The Big West. Here is what you need to know right now, citizens: this government exists purely to parcel up and sell off every natural resource we have to foreign business interests. If you need an example, go to Port Dawkins and look at the water. Maybe you remember when it was clear enough to see the bottom, forty feet down? That was before dredging rights were sold to American mineral companies. Now they want to bring in American cruise ships. We have tried to organize, we have tried to bring resolutions to vote. They turned the military on us and drove us from our homes. Now they call us terrorists. Go look at the water. Remember what you see, and remember who profits from it. It's not you and me, citizens. This is Sister Susie with Dirt Tiger Radio.

***

The storm passed. In its wake, they emerged from shelter and trailed across wet fields, the air swollen with electricity, the sky still smeared with cloud. A lone tree stood next to an algae-covered livestock watering hole, and they gravitated towardit by instinct. Muffled roaring like a distant jet on takeoff came to them as they approached. The tree had an angular gash in its trunk, five feet long and a foot wide, and the inside glowed orange with fire, small flames whipped into vortexes as it hollowed the tree from the inside out. They stared at it in silence.

"Lightning strike," Emma finally said, leaning on her metal detector.

They left it to burn and kept walking.

As they crossed into the perimeter of a village, a small, white postal van drove out towardthem. Mail delivery had once been reliable, but its efficiency, much like everything about The Free State, waned with time.

The van pulled up and idled next to them. The driver, young and bored, rolled down his window. Joshua approached, they talked, and eventually, he emerged with a small packet of identical envelopes, marked with the official Calem government seal, which he distributed to a handful, including Six.

"What is it?" Geoff asked, as Six opened the perforated edge.

Six read the letter and laughed. "You've got to be having me on."

He looked around at the other men reading their letters, their faces a mix of disbelief and anger. Six handed his letter to Geoff.

Geoff skipped over the account information and salutations, and read out loud: "Due to the official change in status of Calem Government's Free State, you are no longer eligible for Active Forbearance on your student loans #001 to #012, totaling C44,650.19." Geoff looked at Six, said, "Holy shit," and continued reading. "Regular monthly payment of C1477.75 will begin again on October 1, and continue until the balance is paid in full. Thank you."

He handed the letter back to Six and repeated, "Holy shit."

***

They spent the day crossing marshes, looking for signs of food. Before sunset, they started to set up camp. Geoff saw a few will-o'-the-wisps, flickers of glowing swamp gas. When he was a boy, he thought they were ghost lamps or evil spirits. He pointed them out to Logan and Six, and they watched the soft blue-green orbs weave and bob in the gloaming.

They sat in silence. The rain held off. A single will-o'-the-wisp, dim green plasma dancing in the shadows, seemed to approach them from the trees.

"Think it's a ghost?" Logan joked.

"Mate," Geoff answered, "if there was a light for everyone who ever died in this jungle, it would never get dark."

The orb flared brightly for a moment, then fizzed away into the night.

The shark man, in his gray suit, came to him that night. He walked Geoff through the jungle to the plane, hovering a few feet above a clearing in a nose-down attitude. Vines and mold grew across the fuselage. "They've been waiting for you," the shark man said.

At the front, through the cockpit windows, he could see figures silhouetted by a dim orange glow. One of them saluted.

"They've been waiting for a very long time," the shark man said.

"Who are you?" Geoff asked him. But he only smiled, his mouth a flat line, eyes dead like a black hole.

***

Clouds are different in the Big West. They obey a strict class system, each remaining in its own strata. High Drifters lording from above, then wispy Flat Ice Thunderheads, Low Scud Runners, and finally the mineral-based Quartz Tumblers, riding beams from the morning sun and skimming along the treetops. Storms bring outsiders, like the green-tinted Squall Kings or Microburst Dandies, temporarily upsetting the architecture of the sky. Much of what happens below in the Big West is dictated by what happens above.

When Geoff was a boy, they told stories of the Big West. The outlaws and gangs who haunted the hills, the fierce jungle cats, crocodiles in the lagoons, and of course, Gaixee Marius, Guardian of the Big West. The last thing anybody who wanders into the Big West ever sees, they said, is Gaixee Marius.

Geoff grew up fascinated by the Big West, afraid of it, entranced by it. They sketched Gaixee Marius, what they imagined he looked like. Like a Bigfoot, Colin Childress said. His uncle claimed to have seen it. Seven feet tall, arms almost as long. No, Trevor Miles said. Not a Bigfoot. A Devil in a red suit.

Geoff's own sketches showed a more human figure, but with a blank face. He wasn't sure what he imagined. Not a monster, not a beast. Something that might approach you as a guide, even a friend, only to lead you to a place you'd never be able to leave.

That, to him, was much more scary.

***

Joshua called the men together. "I had a message last night from those people," he said, and then forced a laugh. He referred to Free State leadership as "those people" or "the arseholes on the hill" or "the Wilshire shitebirds." He started to speak, stopped, and started again, looking depressed. "It's actually from a week ago. I guess somebody at Commerce has decided...we...have an objective. A fucking..." he paused and exhaled. "A fucking mission."

The words hung in the thick morning air. He seemed unwilling to go on, and nobody was willing to prompt him. Finally, he said, "They want us to eliminate the Sister Susie radio broadcasts. They think they've traced her."

"To where?" Emma asked.

"An outpost of some kind. A depot, they think."

The Dirt Tigers had depots throughout the countryside, filled with provisions and supplies they used for themselves and to encourage Free State desertions.

"They want us to what...kill her? Arrest her?" Six asked.

"Nothing like that," Joshua said. "They want us to decommission the radio station."

"So, blow it up," Six said.

"Where is it?" Geoff asked.

"A few miles east of the Baranquilla Salt Flats, they think. Up in the foothills of the Salt Top mountains. Code name Depot 655."

"Sir, that's...east of the salt flats? That's the Big West."

"Yes," Joshua said. "Yes it fucking is."

"We have to walk there?"

"Halfway," Joshua said. "We're meeting a transport unit in Berthshire that'll take us the rest of the way in a couple of UniMogs."

"Is it guarded?"

"They didn't say."

"But, sir....why?"

"We haven't engaged The Tigers since..."

"—since they started feeding us."

"I have two cousins in The Tigers."

"Half the kids I grew up with are with The Tigers."

"Nobody said anything about walking around in the Big West."

"Someone at Commerce is grandstanding," Joshua concluded glumly. "Maybe going to run for President next year. If anybody has the Opt-Out coming up, now might be the time to take it."

The "Opt-Out" was a program designed to enhance enrollment into the Free State. Previously, the minimum commitment had been one year, and nominally, it still was. But after six months, you were given a chance to opt out of your remaining time in the field, with the condition that you would spend the rest of the year working in recruitment or clerical back in Wilshire, at half pay, and then serve an additional year under the same conditions. This had proven wildly popular when first instituted, but word had spread that some of the first adopters had been cycled back into the field within a few months, while others had been subjected to harassment and retribution, and it soon came to be viewed with suspicion. Geoff's Opt Out was a month away. He had not seriously considered it, nor had Logan. Six, however, only three months in, talked about it often.

"What do we do if we run into Tigers before then?" Six asked.

Joshua shrugged. He had never wanted to be in charge. First one squad leader defected to The Dirt Tigers, then another simply walked home, and eventually, he was promoted. His only priority was to keep everybody fed. It never occurred to any of them to conduct anti-Dirt Tigers operations.

They had all heard the Sister Susie broadcasts. In the early days, they'd dismissed or mocked her messages, but she soon began addressing Free State volunteers directly, pointing out with painful accuracy all the broken promises and government propaganda they'd been fed. It became increasingly difficult to discredit her, and while Free State leaders ostensibly forbid enlistees listening to her, it was rarely enforced. Some hardliners still saw her and the Dirt Tigers as far-left extremists, but even Logan, a true believer of the Free State cause, had admitted she "made some good points" sometimes.

Later, Geoff said, "I wondered how long it would take them to go after her."

"What if it turns out it's guarded, and they aren't so keen to let us shut it down?" Six said. "We got people here who never fired a gun in their lives. Like me."

"Yes you have," Logan said. "During basic training."

"No. I just pretended, when everyone else was shooting." He mocked holding a rifle and taking aim. "Pew pew pew."

Later, when the men were asleep, Geoff lay awake. The bush around him seemed darker and closer, like it was folding in on him. He felt deeply conflicted by the mission. He knew the Free State operation was built on lies, and he knew the Dirt Tigers were relatively few in number and posed no threat to society, to say nothing of the times they'd fed them. But as he lay in his hole, he found himself being taken by a simple sense of intrigue. What was out there, in the Big West, where he'd never once been? Was it the half-magical, half-menacing landscape of his boyhood imagination? And Depot 655. What was that? From the moment Joshua had said it, he had thought: maybe it wasn't a mistake to come out here to the mud and mosquitoes. Maybe there finally was a finish line, and having actually accomplished something, he could go back home to Elena, his conscience clear, a little more worthy of whatever she might still feel for him.

Maybe that's what the paisley deer had been trying to tell him.

***

The tall man stands with hands on hips in front of a pub in Darlington, a town on the Jones River. There are only four people inside, sitting together, older men with salted hair and rounded backs. They are drinking and talking loudly as the tall man enters. He stands in front of the bar, examining the drinks menu above it on the wall. The bartender, a thin, bald man with the twitchy awareness of a bird, says, "Drink today, sir?"

"Just a Coke."

He sits alone with his soda while the men behind him talk. He pulls a few documents from his bag, checks his phone.

"Lunch today, sir?" the bartender asks. "There's a special."

"Bring it," he says, without asking what it is.

Within a few minutes, the bartender sets a plate of potted shrimp, mushrooms, and whitebait in front of him. He takes a single bite and loses his appetite. He prods at the shrimp with a fork, absentmindedly stabs at the mushrooms, then remembers he has tracks to cover. He turns to the men behind him.

"Excuse me," he says. "Maybe one of you gentlemen can help me. I'm looking for a red-legged honeycreeper."

"A what?" one man answers, but another man, in a New York Yankees cap, says, "I know what he means. A bird, right?"

"That's right. It's one of the last on my list." He holds up a notepad, but not for long enough for them to read anything written on it.

"Well," the man in the cap says. "I assume you've been to the Middleton Preserve, west of the airport."

"I have. I saw..." he refers to his notepad. "I saw a slaty-tailed trogon there. Also a jacamar. But no honeycreepers."

"You might try going west a bit. Not too far," he hastens to add. "Rainforest gets a little heavier. I expect you'll find everything out there."

He thanks the men and returns to picking at his meal, taking notes in his pad, feeling changes in the humidity and temperature and assessing threats and weaknesses around him with every person who walks through the door.

***

Despite the new mission, the first priority remained food. Even as they started toward the transport rendezvous, they continued to hunt and scavenge in teams of two. Geoff and Logan hiked to a skinny, vegetation-choked stream that wound along the bottom of a narrow valley. They had seen small crustaceans in similar streams, back when they had regular resupply and didn't need to scrounge for food so frequently. But after an hour of prodding in the shallow water, they had found nothing.

"Looks like it's bananas again," Logan said.

"We need protein."

"We should be glad for bananas." Logan trudged out of the stream and shook water from his trouser legs.

Geoff signaled for quiet. The ground underfoot was firm and he had felt the tiniest tremble. He raised his rifle to his eye and watched the wall of vegetation at the edge of the stream. He motioned for Logan to flank him to his right. Geoff put his left palm to the ground and felt another tiny tremor.

Tall grasses rasped together and the vegetation parted. Geoff almost dropped his rifle, such was his surprise. Looking directly at him from a distance of twenty meters was a fully grown tapir, six feet long and at least five hundred pounds.

They had long forgotten about tapir, given them up for extinct in this region. Geoff couldn't even remember the last time he saw tapir tracks, let alone a fully grown adult. They had been subsisting on scraps of rodents, bony stream fish, fruit, and Dirt Tigers charity for weeks. The tapir would be a feast. He was almost afraid to breathe. If it sensed him, it would crash back into the jungle and vanish. But he was upwind, and just far enough away that if he didn't move, it wouldn't see him.

Logan was still behind him and Geoff didn't know if he had seen the tapir; it was his shot. The animal sniffed at the air and took one hesitant step further into the clear, towardthe stream. Geoff could see the muscles in its right shoulder begin to flex as it started to take another step, but then it stopped, its black eyes locking on his own. It could not have survived this long, after all the others had been killed, unless it was exceptionally sensitive and wary, and Geoff knew it sensed trouble. He had already drawn a bead, an easy shot at a large, stationary target. Just before he squeezed the trigger, he imagined the excitement of the other men, the succulence of the roasted flesh, the caloric bounty.

He fired, shots blurting, tearing the air and the vegetation. The rifle recoiled unexpectedly, kicking him off balance, and he knew instantly he'd made a grave mistake. He heard the tapir snort. He ran after it, waving Logan to follow him, but it was gone.

He had missed.

He had meant to fire a single shot, but in his trembling hunger and fatigue, had forgotten to switch the setting from fully automatic. The bullpup rifle was far less accurate in fully automatic mode, but even allowing for that, he was astounded that he could have missed. He kept looking down at the selector switch, toggling it back and forth between single shot and automatic. Logan caught up to him and saw what Geoff was doing.

"You wounded him," Logan said after a pause. "We should track him"

"There's no blood on the grass."

"You could have got him in the haunch. That thick meat wouldn't bleed right away."

"No. I missed. He's gone."

They walked back to the stream and resumed poking through the shallow water. Logan eventually found a few freshwater prawns. Geoff hacked some bananas and cohune dates from the trees, and they started back to camp.

"I can't believe I forgot to switch to single fire."

Logan stopped, forcing Geoff to face him. "It was just a mistake. Everyone makes them. If you dwell on it, you'll make another. It's like a goalkeeper. If he lets in a goal, he can't think about it, or he'll let in others. He has to think only of what comes next."

Thank God, Geoff thought. Thank God she has no way of finding out about this.

That night he dreamed again of the plane and woke with panic in his throat, unable to draw a breath. He felt as if he were choking, dying, right in front of the others. Joshua, awake, saw him sit up. Geoff was embarrassed; he put his hand over his mouth, pretending to yawn, and with great effort he expanded and then constricted his chest, forcing a mighty cough. Air rushed from his lungs and for a moment he feared he would not be able to draw a new breath, but at last his muscles unclenched. He breathed deeply through his nose a half-dozen times, nodded at Joshua, and walked a few paces into the trees to piss. Releasing his bladder brought more relaxation. He could laugh at the dream now, just some image that had got stuck in his head somehow and was replaying night after night. He'd never even flown on a plane. It didn't mean anything.

***

The tall man watches from the bush, pressed deep into grass low to the ground, ignoring the heat and insects. He watches them sitting around their fire, talking, laughing, getting up to relieve themselves in the trees. There is nobody on watch. What his employers told him looks to be true: these people are not interested in confrontation with the Dirt Tigers.

He sends a message on his satellite phone, shielding the light from the glowing screen with his hand.

Heat lightning flashes silently in towering clouds. He watches. After a time, the forest seems to give in to him, and folds him into its dark greenery. The forest is always trying to take me back, he thinks. This time, he lets it.

He moves away silently, like a shark cruising through the valleys of a reef. He has a long way to go.

***

Sometimes, the plane just hung in the air, motionless.

The engines still hummed. Clouds drifted by the windows. A bird alighted on the wing. But the earth lay fixed below them.

"We aren't moving," he finally said.

The shark man looked up from his magazine. "You're right; we aren't."

"We're supposed to be moving," Geoff said. "Even I know that."

The sky grew dark. Below them, lights blinked on, tracing streets and coastlines. It seemed to Geoff that they were higher now, much higher, somehow.

"Did we go up?"

The shark man shrugged.

"What's your name?" Geoff asked him. The shark man only demurred.

They flew on, or hovered on, in silence for quite a while.

"I thought you wanted to go home?" the shark man finally asked.

"Nobody's going anywhere," Geoff answered. "We're not moving."

"But don't you want to go home?"

"You said I couldn't."

"I don't make the rules. People always get that part wrong. I do what I'm told."

Geoff turned away. Outside his window, the earth had receded. Around them were columns of nebula, hanging like the tendrils of water lilies in the black of space.

***

September 1, 1859
Great Inagua Key, Bahamas

The Carrington Event

On these flat islands with unimpeded horizons, sunrise is sudden and dramatic, announced by saturated bars of light streaming across the warm tropical sky. But long before dawn on this late summer night, the sky comes alive. Great curtains of red, green, and purple wave and dance beneath the stars, brighter than a full moon, bright enough to cast shadows under shorebirds hunting in the shallows. Obeying instinct, iguanas emerge from rocks and peer at the light. Bright as it is, it brings no warmth, and they return to hide and await the sun.

In Hawaii, in Cuba, in tropical places around the world, full auroras blaze through the night. People stand and watch in amazement. Those who have traveled know: these are the northern lights. But this is not the north.

Telegraph operators puzzle as their systems begin to fail, or overcharge, giving them electric shocks even after they disconnect the batteries. The world, only newly connected by this technology, returns to silence.

In England, amateur astronomer Richard Carrington sees the aurora and hears the reports of its global propagation, and he thinks he understands. Earlier that afternoon, he had watched his solar telescope in astonishment as it projected enormous sunspots onto a screen, and then, after just five minutes, watched the sunspots as they were consumed by arcs of blinding white light. Some kind of unimaginably massive storm on the surface of the sun. He had never seen anything like it, just as he had never seen the aurora in London, and certainly not in high summer. It could not be a coincidence. He reported the connection to the scientific community, who required no small amount of convincing.

It became known as the Solar Storm of 1859. Or simply, the Carrington Event.

What would a similar storm do today, to a planet dependent on communications and weather satellites, and airplanes, and radio waves?

Richard Carrington won the Gold Medal of the Royal Astronomical Society in 1859, and, five years later, the Lalande Prize of the French Academy of Science. He died in 1875, after a short illness, just forty-nine years old.

***

Joshua couldn't get anything but static on his radio. He took three others with him and set out to find a clearing for better reception. "We'll be right back," he said.

Emma waited a minute and then snorted. "They're not coming back."

"You think?" Logan asked.

"He doesn't want this mission," Emma said. "He talks about it all the time. Just walking back home."

They waited, an hour, two hours. "Damn," Logan said.

Geoff felt his fingertips go numb. He clenched and unclenched his fists. His head began to throb.

"We need more water," he said.

Emma nodded. Six slapped at a mosquito. The others said nothing and didn't move.

"We need more water," Geoff said again, after a few silent minutes.

***

When the sun rose, there were only four: Geoff, Logan, Emma, and Six.

At some point the previous day, exhausted and dehydrated, Geoff had temporarily lost awareness of his surroundings. He slipped into a walking coma and just pressed on. He was vaguely aware of pounding in his head, pain in his feet and legs, clouds of mosquitoes alighting on his face. He remembered a debate, some wanting to go one way, some the other. Geoff knew the "debate" was just an excuse for those who wanted to desert, and they did. Then it was just the four of them. They decided to keep walking northwest, to get clear of the jungle, however long it took. They found a small stream and drank until bloated. With the first ray of morning sun, the fog in his head lifted. With it came clarity.

"We're supposed to be at the pickup in Berthshire in two days," Geoff said. "We can take a short rest, but we need to pick up the pace."

"The pickup?" Six said. "Look around, mate. There's only four of us."

"Nobody's stopping you if you want to desert," Geoff said.

“I’m not quitting,” Logan said. “I’m counting on the student loan forgiveness.”

“Oh my God mate, don’t be a sucker,” Six said.

“If you do the full year, they said—”

“I know what they *said*. You saw the letters we got.”

“I’m still not quitting. We’re not all Marxists.”

“Oh my god,” Six said.

Emma said, “I’m not taking the Opt Out. It’s a scam. I’ll do my year and then go home for good.”

“Clearly, you’re all insane,” Six said.

Geoff looked around. They were still deep in primary jungle. There was no footpath or animal trails. “Okay. Short rest. Then we keep going.”

Geoff sat on a rotting tree blown over by a long-forgotten storm. Green parrots burst from a tree branch and flew away through an opening in the canopy. Something had startled them. He cradled his rifle lightly in his hands and snuck a glance at Logan, who lay with eyelids drooping from fatigue. Something moved in the grass. His lips went dry and he licked them. For a minute it was silent. The lack of sleep, the pain, whatever was continuing to cause the pounding in his head. He couldn’t remember the last real food he’d eaten. He craned his neck and it exploded in a series of alarming pops.

Only silence. Nothing was there.

The rains had continued drubbing the jungle day after day, rinsing color from the sky, and now a morning storm began to moan and rise. The wind freshened and sent a chill through Geoff that didn’t go away. His headache spiked, blurring his vision for a moment. He stretched out his jaw muscles, which had been knotting and twitching for hours.

"Well, I don't know what I'm supposed to do now," Six said. "I'm stuck here with you zealots, and I promised my mother I wouldn't die."

"That was dumb," Logan said.

"Stand up for your country!" Six said. "Stand up for freedom! Smash the Dirt Tigers! I mean a lot of their ideas are good, and they're the only ones with any food—"

"Okay," Logan said. "We get it."

The storm rumbled again, closer, with more menace than the dull monotony of the seasonal rains. A band of blue-gray cloud curled over the jungle, its leading edge sharpened by wind: a squall line, crackling with electricity. Geoff looked up at it. Not a big storm, just a little finger of cloud that would soon pass.

Geoff stood, knowing they would feel obligated to follow, and as he did, some part of him realized he did not want this. He did not want to be in charge, be a "leader." He knew he had absolutely no natural facility for it, and when required, he had always just faked it. But he also knew he wanted to go to Depot 655. Because only then could he go home.

***

International Weather Service Advisory
1 AM EDT MON April 24

Hurricane Selene Approaching Central American Coast

Hurricane Selene wobbling in path towardCentral American peninsula. Tropical storm force winds lashing southern coast of Jamaica.

A hurricane warning is in effect for all of the Yucatan Peninsula and the coasts of Belize, Calem, Honduras, and Nicaragua. Mandatory evacuations have been ordered for outlying islands in Selene's possible path, including Ambergris Caye, Caye Caulker, Roatan, Utilla, and the Miskito Cays. A hurricane watch is in effect for the Yucatan coast of Mexico.

By 1 AM EDT the center of the eye of Selene was moving through the Cayman Trench about two hundred miles SSW of Kingston, Jamaica. Selene is moving towardthe SW at eighteen mph. An increase in forward speed is expected today (Monday). Landfall is expected in the early morning hours of Thursday.

Maximum sustained winds are ninety-five mph with higher gusts. Selene is a Category Two hurricane on the Saffir-Simpson scale. It is expected to strengthen.

Storm surge flooding in coastal areas of nine to seventeen feet above normal are expected if Selene makes landfall without substantial weakening. Selene may produce additional rainfall accumulation of five to ten inches inland across Central America. Widespread flooding is expected.

Outer bands of circulation, bringing high winds, lightning, strong rain, and the potential for tornadoes, will begin moving over the coast and inland on Tuesday.

A following intermediate advisory will be issued by the National Hurricane Center at 3 AM followed by the next complete advisory at 5 AM.

***

Hi Geoff,

The elections are this week. Governor, Mayor, and a bunch of smaller ones. I know you don't care about politics. I never did, either. But it's different in the city. People know these things. I think the choice for Governor is easy. Huddlestone accepted payoffs from the American franchises, so he has to go. But for Mayor and the others, I'll have to do some research. The Dirt Tigers have proxy candidates at the local level. I know that's a sensitive topic, so I'll leave it at that.

It's so amazing, on the nights I stay at the apartment, to wake up in the city. There are always people up, no matter how early. There is a coffee truck in the park. I get a coffee and a donut, and then I sit by the dog run and watch the dogs playing. Every day, there is a Great Dane there so big that he can put his front feet on the top of the fence. Five feet high, at least. His name is Roosevelt. But he's gentle. Some of the smaller dogs actually pick on him, and Roosevelt just lets them, even though he could swallow them all whole.

It's hard to be around my father now. He complains all the time. I don't think he ever learned how to be happy. I don't think we give enough credit to the older generation, the ones who grew up in England, how much they suffered when they were young. It wasn't like it is now. They didn't have hobbies, they didn't get to have fun. I try to remember that. But, if I worry about him too much, I might turn out just like him.

Last time you emailed you said something about requesting a leave. Did it come through? It's very frustrating talking to you like this. I don't know when you will read this, or be able to reply.

I am at the house for the rest of the week. I'll go back to the city on Friday. I count the minutes until I can get there, and then once I'm there, I try to make time stand still.

Stay safe,
Elena

***

Geoff was finding it harder to focus his thoughts on the present. His headache, close to unbearable, and the cramping of his shrunken stomach, caused him to spin away in time. Now he was with Elena, before the Free State, smelling her neck, running his hands down her back, before she twisted away, smiling. He was gone only a few seconds. He pinched violently at the skin in the crook of his arm, hoping to feel the pain above his churning headache. There had been a brief cloudburst when the morning storm had passed overhead, but they had managed to drink and collect only a little.

He heard Six sit up and shuffle closer. In dim starlight, Geoff could see his face, young and still round despite his emaciated frame. The wind stirred and lightning flashed silently.

"Have you ever considered what you actually have against the Dirt Tigers?" Six asked.

"I never said I have anything against them," Geoff said.

"But you enlisted."

"So did you."

"That's different," Six said. "I didn't have a choice."

Lightning flashed again, followed this time by the faintest burble of thunder. Logan flipped from his left side to his right, but didn't wake.

"What makes you think I had choices?" Geoff asked.

Six laughed. "You're personable. Good-looking. Tall. People like you. You could've done anything. You probably even had a girlfriend."

Geoff winced, then rallied. "I'm not smart," he said. "My options weren't as good as you think."

"Nobody's really smart," Six said. "Smart doesn't matter. You can learn anything from books or YouTube. What matters is people liking you. You can't learn that, you either have it or you don't. People like you. And I make people uncomfortable."

Geoff tried to object, but Six cut him off.

"It's okay," he said. "It doesn't matter. We're both here now. God help us. I don't believe in God, but you know what I mean."

Geoff put a hand over his face. "I wish I could sleep," he said.

Insects creaked and chirped, and occasionally a breeze rustled the waxy leaves. Geoff could smell himself, sweat and mud and his rotting boots. He reached for mosquito repellent, but when he pushed the tab, it only spritzed a few drops and then hissed air sadly.

"What did you mean, you don't believe in God?" Logan asked in the dark.

"I don't believe in any of it," Six said. "God, Satan, the Bible, Heaven and Hell. None of it."

Rain finally came. They collected and folded palm fronds to funnel water into their mouths. It fell for only a few minutes, but hard enough so that they could drink until sated.

"See?" Logan said. "God provides. I prayed for rain."

"Pray for food, then," Six said. "Pray we get paid. Pray we can all go home."

"The big man doesn't like when I ask for more than one thing at a time," Logan said.

Logan and Six fitted themselves into the ground. Emma slept leaning against a tree. Geoff's headache kept him awake. He stared up into the dark sky, watching spent rain clouds drift above the trees. He saw three shooting stars in quick succession, and wondered what cosmic mechanisms had sent them to die in the sky. He'd probably learned it in school once, but school felt like a very long time ago.

***

The wind rose and branches began snapping off and knifing into the ground and Geoff understood this was not just another storm. They rushed to gather fallen palm fronds and wedged them together at the base of a kapok tree before crawling under. The wind dropped for a moment and then gusted with a jet engine shriek and tore apart their little shelter. They scrambled after the fronds, but it was hopeless. The rain came in sideways, pelting them like a flurry of punches. Geoff grabbed them each and pulled them close, huddled them together like a rugby scrum, heads down, arms locked. Lightning stabbed through the trees. They dug their heels into the wet earth and leaned against the wind. In another flash of lightning, Geoff saw the sky, greenish-black like a rotten banana and swirling so low he thought it would suck the tops from the trees.

He began to shiver as driven rain and wind sucked the heat from his starving body. He clenched his jaw to stop his teeth from clattering. He looked at Logan and saw his jaw also knotted. Six and Emma had their heads down.

Then, because he couldn't help it, Geoff began to think about what would happen next. It was already bad enough. Now this. Flooding, mass desertions, disease. He wondered what it was like back home.

Despite the chill of rain, his face burned with a kind of fever. He felt one of his back molars grind and crunch under the strain of his knotted jaw. The storm drove against them into the night. They shifted positions, found a little bit more shelter behind a pair of thick mahogany trees, squatted and flexed to stave off the cold. Trees cracked and fell in the jungle, and there were times Geoff was scared, both for himself and for Elena and her farm. They would have had plenty of warning, he thought. They would have evacuated to higher ground.

The storm operated with mechanical efficiency, without malice, merely expending the energy the overwarmed ocean had given it, seeking neutrality, seeking balance. Logan stood when the wind shrieked its loudest. He stretched and shook water from his short hair, looked at Geoff and shouted something that was lost to the wind. Geoff shook his head and Logan mouthed "hurricane."

No shit, Geoff thought.

***

Daybreak brought only a reluctant smudge of light. The wind and driving rain blurred the sky and trees into a chopped mix, and a persistent, low-register echo rang through the jungle. There were long stretches of the night and morning that Geoff could not account for. He slept standing up, perhaps, or simply stood open-mouthed, not really seeing or hearing anything, time slowing and then rushing around him as if driven by the storm. They collected water, but had had no real food, no proteins or sugars, for too many days to remember. Periods of lucidity were interspersed with hours of slack-jawed weaving. Geoff gradually came out of one of these periods to find that the hurricane had passed. The sky was still bruised, but towering black cloud had given way to sheets of rain-fattened gray. He was astonished by the sudden scope of the sky. The jungle canopy had been torn apart like a child's birthday present wrappings, and they saw the entire sky above them. Areas of forest the size of soccer pitches lay flattened, with one or two resilient tropical hardwoods still standing. Fallen trees, branches, and torn fronds covered the ground. Animal trails, trod for decades, were now awash in detritus. Streams and tributaries had been re-routed or choked to death by debris and sediment. The jungle Geoff had known was gone.

He found himself speaking almost automatically. "Ready to go?" he asked.

"Still?" Six asked.

"Are we going to do this every day?" Geoff asked, closing his eyes and wincing with the spasms in his head. "I'm not deserting."

"It's not deserting if we don't have communications," Six insisted.

"He's right," Emma, eavesdropping, added.

Geoff fiddled with his handheld radio again. It had picked up nothing but static since the storm. He stood and shielded his eyes. Even the dim slate sky made him squint. A wave of nausea gripped him and he coughed twice, struggling to stop his head from spinning. He knew Six was right. But leaving now would feel like failure. It would make the years spent in the jungle pointless.

"I can't go back yet," he said. "You guys can leave. I understand."

"Why is this suddenly important?" Emma asked.

Geoff didn't answer, but Six did. "He's trying to impress someone who's not even here."

Geoff didn't have the energy or will to debate. They stood looking at each other for a moment. "Well," Logan said. "It can't hurt to go to Berthshire and see if the transport is there. There'll be food there anyway."

"You just want to meet Sister Susie," Six said. "Admit it."

"Yeah, maybe she'll sign my copy of *The Communist Manifesto.*"

It was an agreement that satisfied nobody, but it was an agreement. They took their bearing from the sun, a moldy spot in a bloated sky, and started moving west. They were slowed by fallen branches and fronds and other debris, as well as their hunger and exhaustion. The edges of Geoff's field of vision flickered rhythmically, and at times shapes appeared as if projected, and then vanished. They walked on.

***

Hi Geoff,

I got the email about your dreams. Freaky. I don't have a clue what they mean. I don't think dream interpretation is really a science, anyway. I think you must have just got an image of a plane stuck in your head.

Flying is a little scary, I have to admit. Once you're in the air it's no problem. You almost feel like you're not even moving. But the takeoff is very, very intense. Fast and loud. It feels unnatural. But once you're up there, the views are incredible. I flew over the Mexican coast once. I could see the reefs offshore, and little beach towns. It was night when we flew home. It might not look like much in the daytime, but Wilshire is beautiful at night. Tiny lights everywhere, gold and orange. Spread out like God took a handful of jewels and flung them across the land.

I'm helping dad today. Gotta go!

Stay safe.
Elena

***

Berthshire is a farming town, surrounded by sugar cane to the north, east, and south, and hemmed in on the west by the protected lands of the rainforest. There is a primary school with a soccer field, a small downtown with shops and a gas station, and a weathered water tower. The town lay along the preliminary plans for a multi-lane highway stretching from Guatemala City to Chetumal in the north of Belize, and rapid expansion was expected. A few banks and American fast food franchises began construction. But then the highway project stalled, never to be restarted, and the banks and restaurants remained in half-built limbo.

The hurricane had left the town strewn with debris, and the main street covered in fine red mud. A dozen workers surrounded a downed power line that was hissing like a viper, which a technician worked to disconnect. Six tried to use his Government PayCard to withdraw money from a corner shop ATM, but the power was out.

A woman approached them, wearing Free State fatigues and carrying a satchel.

"Oh, shit," Six said by way of greeting.

"Nice to meet you too," she said. "Are you supposed to be the squad? Fuck's sake. Four people. Why did you even come?"

"That's a good question," Six said, looking at Geoff. "You're the transport?"

"What's left of it. My name's Marina."

"Where's the rest—"

"They took the UniMog. Just a few hours ago. I went to the bathroom and they left me."

"You had a UniMog?" Logan asked.

"A 419-101. Five liter turbo. Eight speed, six reverse gears. I can get it across anything. Well, I could."

Geoff sighed and scratched his head. "Does anybody have any battery?" he said, holding his dead phone.

"I have battery, but no signal," Marina said. "Haven't had a signal all week."

She handed him the phone, but when he tried to load Maps, he got only a "Searching for Satellites" message, which failed to resolve. He handed it back to her.

"Do you know where it is, at least?" he asked.

"Funny thing about that. I requested satellite images of the GPS coordinates, and I got back five images, each one taken a few years apart. Some of them show a large building. And others show nothing. What's weird is that an early picture shows a building, a later shows an empty space, and then an even later one shows a building again."

"They can put up and take down these depots in an afternoon," Geoff said.

"Yeah," Marina agreed. "Only, the building in these pictures is about three hundred feet long. It's the size of a factory. I can give you the GPS coordinates, but they're just an estimate."

"Nobody said anything about walking there," Six said.

"It's walkable," Marina said. "Take you a few days. And the first few, you're right back in the rainforest. But it's doable."

She gave them the coordinates, and watched, amused, as they argued about whose phone worked the best, and when they might be able to get a signal.

"Everyone's deserting," she said. "All the comms channels went down. It's the Big West. You sure it's a good idea?"

"Oh, it's definitely not," Six said.

"Well," Marina said. "It might be better than heading back towardWilshire. Word is they've got units rounding up deserters all around the city. Charging them with insurrection. Also there's a lot of looting in the small towns. The deserters. Just watch yourselves."

"What are you going to do?" Six asked her.

"I'm linking up with another transport unit. Just as soon as I can get a signal." She waggled her phone, wished them luck, and walked down the street, past the men puzzling over the hissing power line.

Six found a working ATM. They bought bread and fruit and wrapped candies, and by nightfall had eaten most of it.

***

They lost the path after two days, and had to fight through chest-high brush with only Six's small machete. Their progress was so slow that at times it seemed to Geoff that the foliage he slashed grew back before they could clamber through it. After an arduous morning, they finally broke through heavy bush and had easy walking across bare ground for the rest of the afternoon. The sun came through the clouds and it was hot again. Sweat weighted Geoff's shirt and he felt himself slipping in and out of lucidity. Six kept up a steady chatter but Geoff was too weak to object. By evening, they had again been enveloped by heavy jungle.

They lurched along until dark. Geoff had spent much of the day walking with a fog in his head, and several times he had to stop walking to regain his equilibrium. Six accidentally slashed his own forearm with his machete, drawing blood from a shallow but long cut. They had no antiseptic or bandages. He tied an old sock from his small pack around his arm.

Epiphytes and bromeliads shorn by the hurricane littered the forest floor. They gathered handfuls of them and made a makeshift mat. A thin moon rose and diffused just enough light for Geoff to see his own feet. He was tired and wet, but as the air cooled he felt a kind of exhilaration. He was sure they would make it out of the jungle tomorrow. Beyond that was the Big West and Depot 655.

Logan settled into the ground. Six propped himself against a tree and let his chin rest against his chest. Emma lay curled on her side, her hands a makeshift pillow.

Because he had loved Elena since they were kids, he had assumed she would love him too when they got older. But it hadn't worked that way. They remained friends, but the harder he tried to impress her, the more she seemed determined to keep him just a friend. He scored goals playing soccer, but she never came to his games. He tried to do well in school, because he knew she was an excellent student, but his mind wandered and he often filled his notebook with nonsense sketches instead of paying attention. When he tried to talk to her, he found that she had an ever-evolving set of interests that he couldn't keep up with: new bands, or books, or a movie she'd seen in the city. He tried to make her laugh, but his humor was crude, the only kind most teenage boys know.

Finally, exasperated, he stopped trying to show off. He walked home from school with her one day, for the first time not wondering what sort of impression he was making, or trying to anticipate what she might find pleasing for him to say or do. They just talked, no jokes or bragging. He spent more time with his other friends, left her to herself more frequently. That's how it went for a few weeks, then months. On the occasions they were together, he noticed she was slowly opening up, telling him the things she thought and felt, and he did the same. Every now and then she took his hand, but never for very long, and once when they parted, she leaned in and kissed him, quick and dry, on the cheek. The next day, she took his hand and didn't let go.

After two hours, he woke Logan and took his spot on the mat of foliage. He did not sleep well, waking frequently. At times, he was aware that Six was also awake, but mercifully chose not to speak. Geoff leaned against the roots behind him. He heard small animals all around: ants and other insects, bats whipping under the canopy, a centipede that came closer to his feet than he would have liked. His mouth tasted of sour metal, an effect of hunger. Still, despite his fatigue and inability to sleep, his exhilaration persisted. He knew it was a symptom of something bad, an adrenalin reaction to starvation or whatever was causing his headaches, but he gave in to it, an ember glowing in his depleted body. He leaned close to Six and listened to his deep, metronomic breathing. Sleeping soundly.

A sound from the depths of the jungle unnerved him. It sounded like the moan of a man in pain. He listened intently and heard it again, this time louder, as if it came from much closer. Logan prodded at him. "I'm awake," he whispered.

They waited, and then it came again, a long, mournful sound, almost melodic. "It's just an owl," Emma whispered.

They heard its great wings flapping above them, and the clattering of branches, before it alighted. They heard it once more, receding into the dark night, and then it was silent. An hour later, Geoff finally slept.

It seemed only a minute, and he woke too exhausted to remember his dreams. The morning divulged fat wet clouds promising rain, and they started walking. They were out of water again. Geoff's throat burned with thirst. He tried to spit but could produce no saliva. They came back into heavy brush. After two hours of slashing and picking their way through the under-story, Geoff began to be troubled by nagging pain in both feet. While taking a turn with the machete, a wet fold of skin tore away from his right hand, softened by persistent sweat, like a half-cooked pancake. Blood welled up under the blister but didn't spill. They rested; he used his knife to cut away a strip of material from the bottom of his shirt, and bound it tightly around his hand.

He was not alone in suffering. A horsefly had bit Logan on the neck sometime during the night, and it swelled badly. He quickly scratched right through it and it erupted angrily.

Six remained cheerful, but his wounded arm hindered him, and he whimpered in pain occasionally. Geoff soon began to limp. He took off his boots and found large blisters on the heels and balls of his feet, angry red wounds like bullet holes in his saturated skin. He cut more fabric from his shirt and bound his feet as best he could.

By late afternoon, even Six's spirits began to flag. Still the clouds withheld rain. But then they found water.

It was more than a stream—a tributary, twenty feet across, probably of the Ocampo River. "We're getting there," Geoff said. "Lake Ocampo can't be more than five miles."

The stream was turbid from the storm and flowed rapidly. They drank from their knees, ignoring the silt.

"We should swim," Six said. "We might find some crayfish."

He plunged in without undressing. Logan took off his shirt and boots and joined him in the tannin-colored water. Geoff, protecting his open blisters, sat on the bank, while Emma removed her boots and waded. Six and Logan dove and surfaced, empty-handed, again and again.

Logan waded to the bank. "There's not shit here," he said, climbing out.

Six took a step to follow him, felt something brush against his leg, and stopped. "Are there snapping turtles?"

"If you stepped on a turtle, grab it," Geoff said.

He started and then stopped again. "Hey," he said, and giggled nervously. "I think there's something down here."

"A turtle? Grab it, asshole!" Logan said.

"It's a lot bigger than a turtle," Six said, just above a whisper.

Geoff, brushing mud off his boots, looked up. "Come on out," he said, as casually as he could.

Six nodded and took another step. He felt the water swirl across his legs, seeming to come from all angles. He took two more steps; he could almost reach out and touch Geoff. The water stilled. He took another step.

"Come on out," Geoff repeated, still calm, reaching out with his left hand.

Six nodded and forced a smile. He took three more steps and reached for Geoff's hand. They clasped, and Geoff heaved him up onto the bank.

They stood looking at the flat brown water for a few moments, until Geoff spotted a trail of fine bubbles. The water bulged, and then a flat black object popped to the surface. Two eyes poked above the water, looking directly at them from fifteen feet, and then submerged again.

"Holy shit," Logan said.

"Jesus," Six said, a stricken look on his face. "A fucking crocodile?"

"It's not that big, maybe six feet," Geoff said. "Logan, give me the knife."

"What are you going to do?" Six asked.

Geoff thought for a moment. "Where it narrows," he said, pointing down the stream. "Drag some stuff in there. These branches." He gestured at storm-broken trees. "Block him in."

"You want to eat a crocodile?" Six asked.

"The tail is all muscle."

"Wouldn't it make more sense to shoot it?"

"I don't really want to advertise our position out here," he said. Nobody had acknowledged it, but they all knew they were closing in on the Big West now.

The crocodile surfaced again, facing away from them, and began to clamber out of the water on the far bank. It moved slowly, as if it were in pain, and Geoff thought it looked almost fake, like the animatronic puppets he'd seen at a fair in Wilshire once. It heaved itself up the bank and collapsed in gelatinous mud, lying parallel to the stream, thirty feet from where they stood.

The croc exhaled, a long hiss, almost a sigh. It was little more than a leathery bag covering a skeleton. They could see the outlines of its ribs, and the knobs of its spine. It was covered in old scars that had healed as raised white lines. It hissed again, weakly, like air indifferent about escaping a leaky balloon.

"It's starving," Six said softly.

Geoff sighed and handed the knife back to Logan. They stood watching the croc for a few moments. Six looked down at the crayfish in his shirt. "Can I—"

"Go ahead," Geoff said, anticipating the question. "But just a few."

Six underhanded a crayfish towardthe croc, but it fell short and plopped into the water. The croc didn't react. Geoff held out his hand, and Six gave him a crayfish. His toss was true; the crayfish landed right next to the croc. It slowly tilted its head and pinched at it with its jaws. Eventually, it worked the small crustacean into its mouth. For the next few minutes, Geoff threw half a dozen crayfish. It ate the first three, but let the rest plop into the mud without moving.

"If it's going to die anyway," Logan said. "Shouldn't we—"

"No," Geoff said. "Leave it in peace."

Six patted Geoff on the shoulder. They started to leave. The crocodile shifted, as if it was trying to look back at them as they left, and then slumped back into the mud. They heard it hiss again. Geoff wondered if it was trying to thank them, or if it had decided it was time to die.

***

He had gone on leave once without telling her. Wilshire University Athletics Club, the city's top professional soccer team, but a relative minnow in the big picture of Central and South American soccer, had managed to entice Argentinian giants River Plate to play a friendly match to inaugurate their new stadium. Logan, improbably, scored a pair of tickets from a cousin, and their two-day leave request was just as improbably approved.

He knew he should have told her. She wouldn't have minded. She would, in fact, have been happy for him, and wouldn't have expected him to cram a visit to Margaret Town into a short leave. But for whatever reason, he didn't say anything, and he swore Logan to social media secrecy.

It's not that he didn't want to see her, or that he was especially excited to go to the game; he couldn't explain it. Even as they watched the game in the sparkling new stadium, packed with singing, swaying masses of fans, he wondered why he hadn't wanted to be honest with her, and in the end, it spoiled his night. Guilt nagged at him like the beginning of an illness, and he was relieved to return to their unit the next day, almost glad he hadn't enjoyed himself more.

What especially bothered him were the moments during the buildup to the game, with streams of fans turning the streets around the stadium into a festival, when he felt an elation that he wanted to share with just one person: Elena. He wanted to tell her about the flares and fireworks people let off, how the traveling River supporters were greeted with friendly songs, and the game itself, both teams defending casually and looking to score spectacular goals. But his befuddling decision meant he couldn't say a word to her about any of it.

***

They followed the flow of the stream, knowing it would lead them to towns or small settlements near Lake Ocampo. Logan trapped a dozen crayfish in the muddy shallows and they ate them raw. The effect of the small meal was almost immediate; the proteins and sugars in the crayfish blood acted like fresh rain on parched mudflats, reviving their flagging limbs, quickening their pace. Geoff's headache eased, though he was still hobbled by his blisters.

Squall lines of mosquitoes jabbed at them from above. They continued along the stream, now widening. Another tributary joined it from the north, and the current increased. Six had to raise his voice above the sound of rushing water.

"I'm not very successful with women," Six said. "Can you help me, Emma? I don't understand what they want."

"Paint the house and leave us alone," Emma said.

"I don't know how to paint."

"You've got problems, lad."

Geoff looked ahead. The tributary had turned into a river and was beginning to roar. Another stream fed into it from the north, bringing torrents of rainwater from the hurricane. They had to walk farther from the water, as the rushing current was cleaving chunks of mud from the bank. Ahead they saw a newly formed island, a stand of higher ground that the angry new river had cut from the jungle. Arcs of water like leaping dolphins roared around either side of the bullet-shaped islet, no more than fifty feet long and twenty feet across. A few palm trees, weakened by the storm and increasingly losing purchase to the muddy island, listed like the masts of grounded sailboats. A single ibis stood on the edge, ten feet above the rushing water, tall grass behind it.

"Somebody is there," Six said.

A face peered at them, partly hidden behind a palm tree. They were only fifty feet away but separated by the howling river. The man, realizing he'd been seen, ducked behind the tree.

Six stepped closer to the river and cupped his mouth, but Geoff placed a hand on his chest and said, "Don't."

The man peeked from behind the tree, then withdrew again. A six-foot chunk of his little island broke away and fell into the rushing, foamy water. The ibis took flight.

"But he's stranded," Six said.

"If he wanted our help he wouldn't be hiding from us," Logan said.

Another chunk of the island slid into the river. The man stretched his neck to look over the edge, without stepping out from behind the tree.

"We can't do anything and it's not safe here," Geoff said.

Six waved apologetically at the man. He only stared back.

The pain in Geoff's feet slowed them, even as it seemed they were leaving the heart of the jungle behind and finding easier walking. Logan saw that he was struggling and suggested they rest, but Geoff ignored him and hobbled on.

"It's not right," Six said. "We should have offered to help him."

They pushed away from the river, through low scrub covered in a fresh mudflow. Geoff put a hand to his forehead. Something was happening—his vision narrowed and he began to see concentric rings of flashing lights in front of his face. The dark forest began to shimmer in their glow. His muscles unclenched, and warmth spread through his limbs and down his back, along with a peaceful sense of well-being. His blisters stopped hurting, and the cramps in his abdomen released like a small dam bursting. He felt rested and well-fed. But then his vision clouded over and the pain returned. Geoff stopped and looked at Logan. He felt it must be obvious that there was something wrong with him.

"Did you hear that?" Logan said.

A groaning sound came through the forest, deep and grainy and fading away to a series of clicks, before starting again. They looked around; it was coming from the ground at their feet.

"What is it?" Six asked.

An overturned giant land crab squirmed slowly on its back, its large pincher claw waving ineffectually. Seeping green mud seemed to be engulfing the crab. Geoff reached his foot forward to dislodge it with his toe, and then recoiled. It wasn't green mud swallowing the crab, but an enormous toad, the size of a coconut. It had the crab's rear legs in its trap-like mouth, pulling it further into its maw and groaning with each contraction. The crab, still alive, offered no resistance. Neither animal took any notice of the people standing above them. The toad's muscles rippled under its oily skin. One of the crab's legs snapped off.

Geoff stood staring at it. The others had already continued down the trail.

***

The tall man looks across a storm-flattened landscape in morning sun. His eyes flick right and left, focus, shift, move on. There are many tracks. They radiate like the spokes on a bicycle wheel. He finds the track that he knows is the right one, and follows it, like a hunting dog on a scent, or a fire ant awakened from a disturbed mound. He already knows he'll find what he's looking for. Then the landscape flickers for a moment, and he is forced to confront doubt.

All things converge in the end, he thinks.

He shakes his head to clear his vision, and resumes his track.

***

Hurricane Selene whirls into the mountains and begins to die, the jagged karst slopes shearing away organized swirls of cloud, tearing apart the eye wall. Cut off from the heat of the ocean, the storm fractures, vents its energy, and falls across the mountains as a drab mass of gray mist, no longer even a tropical storm. It's over. In its wake, birds circle in confusion, old navigational guideposts gone, and at the shore, sandbars shifted by the storm surge paint a new coastline.

For now, the ocean is flat and calm and hot. There will be more storms. The land is torn and still saturated, its people blitzed and dazed by nature and violence, reeling as if from an expertly delivered jab, defenseless now against a knockout blow.

***

They walked in rain and blinding sun, in unbearable heat, in misty morning chill. Geoff's raw blisters erupted and scabbed over and erupted again. They found an abandoned village and an overturned car, but nothing to eat. Rainwater kept them moving. They rarely spoke.

Geoff's headache worsened. He had dizzy spells and visions of flashing lights more and more frequently. He had hot flashes followed by chills. He thought he saw Elena, and then yes, there she was. She wanted to help him. She offered to carry his rifle, tried to support his bulk on her shoulder as they walked.

"You'll be home soon," she said.

It was good to see her, to have her there, feel her skin and smell her hair. But he couldn't talk to her. He didn't know why not. But she didn't seem to mind.

A dog began following them on the margins of another village. It was small, twenty pounds at most, with matted, rust-colored fur and ears that stood straight up, as if it were perpetually startled. Six coaxed it close and petted it for a few moments, and it trotted alongside them as they followed the narrow road across flat, grassy plains. Storm clouds clumped above them.

"The heavy hitters are moving into place," Geoff said, looking up at the clouds. It was something his father had always said in the face of a building thunderstorm. Saying it now took effort and left him winded.

The air was humid and absolutely still. The dog led the way, and they were glad for it.

***

This is Sister Susie with Dirt Tiger Radio. The radio waves are acting strange, but we're still here. Did you know our government receives millions of dollars in international aid after natural disasters like hurricanes? Do you think any of it actually reaches the people who need it? Where do you think it goes? I think you know the answer to that. There are more storm clouds ahead. Stay safe, citizens. This is Sister Susie with Dirt Tiger Radio.

***

"I had this dream," Six said. "It's our unit, but it's not, really. None of you are there. We go into a little village. We've been in the jungle forever, we're covered with mold and vines, there are leaves growing right out of our ears, but now we're coming back to the world. And we're jubilant, really, singing and carrying on, and all the locals are out there to greet us, like we're heroes."

"Like what they told us would actually happen," Emma said.

Geoff rubbed his temples. Six picked at the rancid sock tied around his wounded arm and cleared his throat before he continued.

"That's right. But then I realized the villagers weren't greeting us. They didn't even see us. They were like holograms. You could see right through them. They were bug-eyed, staring, but they couldn't see us. They were phantoms. Ghosts. And everyone in my unit, they started walking through them, and each one stopped in front of a different phantom and just stared right back at it. I had a feeling, then, that one of the phantoms, way at the back, was waiting for me, so I started walking back there, and I could see this ghoul face sort of leaning around the others, looking at me. When I finally got to him, I couldn't really see his face. His head kept turning away from me. I started to speak to him but when I did, he began to giggle. A mean, sniveling little giggle. I started to walk away and the ghoul spoke, just a mumble. I had to lean close to hear. He was chanting, like the way you do when you're a kid and singing some stupid kid's song. He just kept chanting."

"What was he saying?" Geoff asked.

"He was saying, '*One down, two to go, three altogether, go kill Joe.*' Over and over. I didn't know what it meant, so I asked him, but he just repeated it: '*One down, two to go, three all together, go kill Joe.*'

"I started to feel panicky and walked away. Another guy, he was standing in front of his ghoul trying to make it laugh. He was doing a vaudeville dance, singing '*Hooray for HOLLYwood, la-la-la-laaaa-la-la*' really loudly, a big grin, the whole thing. And the ghoul just stared. '*Hooray for HOLLYwood*! Hey, c'mon mate! Laugh!' When he saw me he said, 'These lads have no sense of humor!' He was red-faced and sweaty from the effort. Then the squad leader came by and grabbed us and we walked out of there, walked back to the jungle, all the ghouls watching."

Six stroked the dog at his feet, whispering to it as it slept.

"It's just a dream," Logan said.

“You want to know what I think happens after you die? You go to that village and you stand there, forever. A ghoul.”

Six whispered again to the sleeping dog.

Geoff pressed his palms against his closed eyes. Headache tore at the inside of his skull.

“Or maybe you just walk forever,” he said through the pain.

***

The sickness lurking in Geoff finally took hold. A dull, nauseating ache radiated from the bones in his upper back, down into his hips, and finally his legs, which somehow kept moving. He saw only a few feet in front of him; the rest was lost to a blinding white haze. He stopped thinking, just walked, didn’t worry if the others noticed something was wrong. Skin pulled free from his heels with every step, but the pain didn’t slow him. It was Logan who wanted to rest first.

“Let me check your temperature,” Elena said, reaching with a slender arm and cupping his forehead with her palm. She frowned. “You’re burning up.”

“I’m okay,” he said, just a whisper.

She smiled sadly at him.

“That’s a new dress,” he said.

She shook her head. “No, it’s not.” She crouched down beside him and looked up at the trees. “It’s pretty out here.”

“Is it?” He tried to look up, but even the overcast sky blinded him. He put his hands to his eyes.

“You need to rest, that’s all. You can’t keep going like this.”

"No." He shook his head. "I can keep going. I can take anything."

"But not this?"

"Anything."

She looked at him, tried to smile. "There is no value in this."

He didn't respond, just reached out and touched her hair. She checked his temperature again.

"You have malaria," she said.

"Maybe just flu."

"Do you have medicine?"

"We ran out," he answered. "Last year."

She took his hand. "This should be obvious, but...it's no good if you die." He looked at her and saw worry in her eyes. "Everything is changing," she said. "You'll come home some day and see."

A shadow crossed his face and she was gone. He tried again to look at the sky, and this time he wasn't blinded by pain, though his vision was still narrow and blurry. He rose to his feet, stretched his arms above his head, his joints and spine popping. The pain made him queasy, but he fought off the retch and looked at Emma, Logan, and Six, sitting cross-legged in the grass. As sick as he was, they were waiting for him to tell them what to do.

Far behind them, industrial power lines strung between enormous skeleton towers draped through a crease of the valley. He pointed towardthem.

"Let's go," he said.

***

In the growing gloom of twilight, they saw filaments of colored light through the trees and heard soft chiming bells and the laughter of children. They emerged into a grassy clearing shrouded in mist, in the center of which was a small amusement park, like a county fair or traveling circus.

"Sure, why not," Six said.

A miniature ferris wheel, two stories high with six passenger cars festooned with colored string lights, turned languidly, each car empty. Arranged around it in a circle were a dozen old railroad boxcars serving as games booths or food cars, also strung with lights. The chiming bells and laughing children they'd heard were being broadcast on a recorded loop. Surrounding everything was a miniature train, moving slowly around the perimeter of the park. It, too, was empty.

Geoff led them into the park, stepping over the narrow tracks as the miniature train trundled past, and the recorded chiming bells and laughter grew louder.

"There has to be somebody here," Six said. "Right?"

Geoff walked over to the ferris wheel. "That might get just high enough to see over the trees. Figure out where the hell we are," he said.

"It doesn't look that safe," Logan said, stepping closer, but Geoff ignored him. He looked for a start-stop lever or button but couldn't find any operating mechanism at all. The cars moved slowly enough for him to time it, and he hopped in one as it passed and rose with it slowly above the tree line. He stood up as much as the undersized car would allow, and for ten seconds had a view further into the valley. He thought he saw more lights ahead through the trees. Then the car descended.

"One more time," he said to the others as the car revolved past them and began to climb again, almost reluctantly. But just before he reached the apex, the machinery hissed and the wheel stopped. Momentum caused the car to rock back and forth a few times.

"Who pushed a button?" Geoff called down.

"Nobody touched anything," Six said.

Around the park, systems began shutting down. The string lights turned off on the wheel. The little train stopped, and the recording silenced. "I think you should get down from there," Emma said in a tone which suggested she was trying to stay calm.

"I agree," Six said.

The car wobbled and then hung motionless. Geoff could see further down the valley now, to the lights ahead he'd only glimpsed before. It was another amusement park, identical to this one. His vision sharpened and seemed to zoom in. It wasn't merely identical; it was the same park, and they were standing in it, Logan and Emma and Six, and he was approaching the ferris wheel and waiting for the right moment to step into a car.

"Come down," Emma repeated.

Beyond the amusement park, in the deepest trench of the valley ahead, he saw a jungle cat lying in wait, hidden by thistle. Then his perspective zoomed back out, it all faded into the distance and looked as it should, and the second amusement park was gone.

"Come on."

Geoff climbed down the structure, noticing as he did that it was bolted together with mismatched hardware and joints that wobbled as he gripped them. He reached with his right foot for a final step before dismounting, but a support strut gave way and he tumbled the final five feet to the ground, landing with an undignified gasp of escaping air. Logan rushed to make sure he was okay, then laughed once he realized he was.

"This way," Geoff said, and they followed him out of the park and back toward the forest. Just as they reached the tree line, the recording began playing again, chiming bells and laughing children, and they turned to see all the lights blink back on, and the ferris wheel begin to slowly turn.

***

Geoff was openly feverish, sweating and shivering, sometimes lucid, sometimes in a fog of pain. Logan suffered from blisters and an eruption of infected mosquito bites. Six unwrapped his forearm cut and was so horrified by the sight of the wound—infected and well on the way, Logan said, to gangrene—that he immediately covered it again. Emma was simply tired.

They walked through fields of soybeans and bananas, mostly abandoned and overgrown. The bananas hadn't yet ripened and were tough and inedible. They climbed a hill and from its summit they saw a new stand of rainforest to the west.

"Holy shit," Six said, pointing.

From the forest, people poured in waves, like delayed travelers finally let off a tardy train. "Deserters," Logan said. They moved east through the fields, in clumps and clusters, a few alone. They descended the hill and were among them. A deserter made eye contact with Geoff and came running over.

"Holy fuck," he said, laughing with a complete absence of pity. "What happened to you poor bastards?"

They stood looking at him, in shock at the sudden and unexpected immersion back into some kind of society. The deserter walked over to Six, grinning, flipping open his muddy jacket, nodding at but keeping his distance from Logan and Geoff. He tried to pet the dog, but it backed away from him.

"Where is everyone going?" Geoff asked.

"You don't know, G.I. Joe? New Middlesborough. There's supposed to be food there."

The deserter laughed at them again, then ran to greet another group.

They followed the trudging figures along a dirt road. In the early evening, they passed a group of deserters sitting around the burning carcass of a government Jeep, smoke and sparks streaming up into a red sky. They had a small radio repeating some kind of government message that kept breaking up into static. One of them ran over with a wild grin, but Geoff pushed him firmly away before he could even speak. "What's with this bloke?" the deserter said, laughing.

"He hasn't had his coffee," Six said. "What's going on? Why is everyone deserting at the same time?"

"Not deserting, mate. They opened the Opt-Out to anyone who wants to take it, no matter how many days in you are. This week only. It's the beginning of the end, mate."

"Is that true?"

"It's what I heard."

"Why are they burning that Jeep?"

"Giles from our unit heard that a medic in a different unit said that a friend of his in another unit heard if you get caught in one of your unit's Jeeps, they take the maintenance costs out of your last check."

They kept walking.

New Middlesborough was the last major town in the Big West. Beyond was only tiny villages, jungle, salt pans, and the Salt Top mountain range. It was an easy downhill trek through fields and citrus farms. The orange trees had been picked clean by hordes ahead of them. Opt-Outs bedded down in the grove as the sun began to sink. Some were jubilant and defiant, but many were silent, their eyes vacant with hunger and exhaustion. A small plane flew low over them and circled several times before it banked away, red lights blinking from its wingtips, toward the violet horizon. Vertical lines of smoke rose in the distance. Geoff cradled his rifle as they approached another burning vehicle, smelling of raw fuel and melting plastic. They passed it without stopping.

They should have been close enough to the town to see lights on the horizon, but there were only more streams of smoke diffusing into the twilight vapors. A few rounds of automatic fire blurted in the hills behind them. They agreed to bed down for the night. Not even Six felt like talking. Geoff stared up at the purple sky as it darkened and a few stars emerged. He dug his shoulder blades into the ground. Small fires, scattered like galaxies, flickered in the fields.

He slept, or not. There was the purple sky and grass on his neck and pain exploding from his temples, and Elena again, not talking, just holding his hand and pushing the sweaty hair back from his forehead. Six mumbled softly, pain infecting his dreams. Another plane flew overhead, this time a commercial jet, thirty thousand feet above them. He saw the lights winking before he heard the sigh of the engines, low and mournful and lingering long after the plane had gone. A meteor bisected the sky, then another. Opt-Outs laughed in the distance.

He was lucid but felt the intrusion, on the periphery of his vision and his mind, of something else that wanted in. He shook his head to clear it, and when that didn't work, rubbed his heels ever so slightly against the inside of his boots, inflaming the blisters, igniting more pain. The pain would save him, would keep him grounded to the physical world. It was fine, of course, that Elena came, but not the mists and smoke and flashing lights, nor the shadow figures that walked freely within them.

Some time later, they woke and began walking again. Ahead were squat buildings silhouetted in the red glow of sunrise. The rising sun glared right through some of the windows, back to front, a mosaic of jeweled fire like the multifaceted eyes of a giant insect.

They entered New Middlesborough an hour later. A few dogs ran out to them and stood barking, keeping their distance. Six's dog—he had not yet named it—barked in return, small but defiant. Opt Outs walked the streets, carrying their rifles on the hip, going in and out of every concrete block building. The hurricane had stripped small trees of their leaves and left a swill of muck in the streets. An Opt Out eating an ice cream cone watched them from a third-story window. Six waved and called up to him.

"Where did you get that?"

He withdrew without answering.

Another Opt Out approached them. "The food's in there," he said, pointing to a concrete block of flats across the street, two stories high. "Top floor. But don't go up there unless you have money or something to trade."

They entered the building. The two downstairs flats had been ransacked in a casual way, as if there had been no resistance. Nothing was overturned or broken, but the cabinets were open and empty. The electricity didn't work. In the confined space, Geoff was nearly overcome by his own raw stink, and fought back a gag. Logan heard something and motioned for them to stop. Geoff called, "We're coming up!" toward the upstairs flats.

"Suit yourself," a voice answered.

Geoff nudged open the door with his rifle. Inside, three shirtless soldiers lounged on the floor, half-empty bottles in their hands, and a fourth sat in an overstuffed chair, rifle across his lap. The windows were closed and the heat and stench were overwhelming. A woman sat in one corner. She twirled a strand of her hair with one finger and stared at the floor.

"Weapons down, lads," said the young man in the overstuffed chair. "All of them."

Nobody moved. The man shrugged. "Weapons on the floor or there's no business done."

Geoff nodded at Logan. They lay their rifles in front of them.

"You all taking the Opt Out?" Geoff asked.

The man in the chair dropped his bottle, spilling the remaining contents. They were all drunk. Outside, somebody fired a service rifle a few times in apparent celebration. "I asked if you were taking the Opt Out," Geoff said.

"Isn't everybody?" the man said.

Geoff kicked at the man's bottle, sending it skidding into the wall. The men looked bored. The woman stared at him, still twirling her hair.

"What about food?" Geoff asked.

"What about it?"

"What do you have?"

"MREs. Fifteen C's each. Or you can trade, if you don't have cash." He pointed at their rifles. "Five for each."

"Five MREs for a rifle?"

"They'll keep you alive, mate. Twenty-five hundred calories each. There's nothing left like that out there."

Weapons and clips of ammo stood neatly in one corner. Geoff pointed at them. "What are you going to do with all this?" he asked.

"Trade it on down the line."

"For what?"

"For whatever I need."

"How long you been stealing the MREs? We've been starving in the field for months."

The man sat forward. "You got it wrong, mate. We didn't steal these from you. We stole them from The Dirt Tigers. *They* stole them from you."

Logan didn't look up, but he stepped from behind Geoff and turned ever so slightly toward the three other men in the room, all of them still slumped on the floor. The man with the rifle was looking directly at him.

"Alright," Geoff said. "Let me see the food."

"Marlon," the man said. "Show them."

Marlon, slightly bucktoothed, groaned and started to get to his feet.

"Hang on," Geoff said. Marlon stopped, frowned, and looked back at the man in the chair. "How did you steal them from The Dirt Tigers?"

The man held Geoff's eyes for a moment. "You want the shit or not?" he said. "There's lots who do."

Behind his eyes, Geoff's migraine peaked. In his peripheral vision he noticed Marlon and the other men, while still affecting boredom, had begun to cradle their weapons.

"I just want to know," Geoff said. "How did you steal them from The Dirt Tigers?"

The man didn't answer. Marlon moved slightly closer to the man in the chair. The fourth man, sitting on the sofa with a rifle across his lap, rose to his feet.

"I think you lot should leave," the man in the chair said.

"We're leaving," Geoff said. "But not without food."

"I'm not running a charity."

"You're running a scam."

Logan slowly leaned down and picked up his rifle. Six followed him.

A part of Geoff's brain knew he was bluffing. He could barely see straight, let alone handle a violent encounter with armed strangers. But something told him the man in the chair was bluffing too, and would back down. He had known his share of blowhards before. He took one step forward, slowly extended a hand right past the man's face, and picked up an MRE from a stack on a side table. Nobody moved or said anything. Geoff held eye contact with the man in the chair and methodically took another three MREs. Logan walked over and took another two, handed them to Six, and took two more himself.

The main in the chair glared at him but said nothing.

Geoff retreated a few steps, then turned, and they left the room and walked downstairs and back outside into sunlight.

"Well!" Six exclaimed brightly. "It's the people you meet along the way that makes travel so rewarding."

"Shut up," Geoff said, hiding a smile.

Some time later, having eaten and then struggled to keep down one of the MREs, his vision cleared and the crushing pain ebbed just enough for him to be lucid. They had found an abandoned flat and piled discarded clothes and towels on the floor, where they settled for the night. Geoff felt something in his chest or his stomach, he wasn't sure which, and didn't know what it was. Not a pain, for once, but a growing pressure that seemed to spread his ribcage. He found comfort in squeezing himself around the midsection.

There were no lights, and it was dark—the one small window had been boarded—but, amazingly, when Six plugged his phone into a wall outlet, the screen blinked to life, illuminating the little room. They couldn't get a signal, and the Maps app again displayed a blinking "Searching for

Satellites" message and a spinning hourglass. But the dim artificial light made them all feel better.

They tried to sleep. Geoff rolled onto his side, jabs of dull pain crackling all over his body, his stomach queasy and distended from the oily MRE. "I can't sleep," Six whispered in the dark.

Geoff twisted, trying to relieve the pressure on his neck and back.

"You must be looking forward to seeing her," Six said. "Your girl."

"I am," Geoff said, too weary to plead for quiet. Then he said, "Who said I had a girl?"

A shout came from outside, a *pop* and tinkle of a bottle breaking, and laughter. The sounds faded, and again the night stilled.

"I thought you were going to get us killed back there," Six said.

"I was hungry."

"How did you know he wouldn't do anything?"

"I didn't. I got lucky."

Geoff shifted again, his stomach groaning, nerves firing through his bones like tiny explosions. His mouth was dry—he only just noticed it—and he felt like his throat was trying to stick together and close. He felt the ground shift and his head began to spin, but he stopped it with effort.

"There's something rotten in here," Six said, sniffing at the air. "Can you smell it? God. There must be a dead rat."

"I don't smell anything," Logan said.

"I'm sorry, but we have to find it. I can't sleep with a rotting animal." Six stood and began stumbling around in the darkness. "I can't tell where it's coming from. It's everywhere."

"I don't smell anything either," Geoff said.

Six stopped. "Oh, shit," he said quietly. "It's my arm."

"The bandages need changing, that's all," Geoff said.

"No. My fucking arm is rotting."

"If you don't shut up and go to sleep," Logan interrupted, sitting up, "I'm going to take a shit on your arm."

"Jesus," Six whined in the darkness. "That's a little extreme, don't you think?"

Fatigue overcame them. The glow from Six's phone illuminated the small space until it went into sleep mode. Outside they heard voices, tired feet moving across paving stones, until finally they all slept.

***

Before sunrise, they ate another MRE and started on the road again, leaving town before the Opt Outs—some sleeping or stumbling hungover in the streets—noticed them. Food didn't fix everything. Geoff still had his blisters and his fever. Six cradled his arm. Logan's infected mosquito bites made all movement painful. But they had energy once again, sugar fizzing in their blood, the maddening hollow ache of hunger gone, almost forgotten with one full stomach. The dog skipped ahead, and they kept pace.

A few rounds of gunfire popped from behind them. The rising sun illuminated thick mud and debris from the hurricane, covering the road ahead of them.

Six pulled his phone from his pocket and shielded the screen from the rising morning light. "'Searching for Satellites,'" he read aloud. He looked up at the sky, fuzzy and purple, a few stars still showing to the west. "Are we going to talk about what the fuck happened to the satellites?"

They covered ground easily at first, buoyed by their energy and the relatively easy going of the road. As they descended out of the hills, though, the day grew hot, and hurricane damage became more prominent. They passed a flattened stand of trees, and several times had to venture far into the fields to cross especially deep mud flows. After two hours, pain took a toll and the pace slowed. They had to rest frequently. The top layer of mud began to dry under the hot sun, but underneath the crust it was like raw cake batter, coating their legs and boots, grasping at them, tiring them further. They were mostly alone on the road, the first wave of Opt Outs having stayed in New Middlesborough, but they were following two sets of footprints in the mud that Geoff began to pay attention to.

"He's hurt," he said, pointing at the set of tracks on the left. "His left foot. You can see from the way the tracks are all smeared out, he has to drag it."

They looked ahead. The road and surrounding fields were empty, apart from a few broken or listing trees.

An hour later, the twin tracks converged and became just one.

"What happened?" Logan asked.

"He carried him," Geoff said. "See, the steps are shorter."

They followed the single set of tracks until they saw a figure in the distance on the side of the road. Approaching, they saw it was an Opt Out, sitting on his own on a fallen tree, his rifle across his lap. Six picked up the dog and held it against his chest.

The Opt Out waved at them as they approached.

"What happened to the other one?" Geoff asked.

"What other one?"

Geoff pointed back at the road behind them. "We saw the footprints."

The Opt Out, a little older than most Free Staters, with a patchy beard that failed to cover acne scars, pushed his cap back and wiped sweat from his forehead. He looked at the MREs poking out of Six's rucksack and said, "Where'd you get those? All I've had the last week is bananas. Tried to get something to eat back there—" he pointed in the direction of New Middlesborough. "But I just got beat up." He laughed.

They only stared at him.

"Friendly guys, huh?"

"What happened to the bloke you were walking with?" Geoff asked.

"I just buried him, if you want to know," he said. "We both got the shit beat out of us back there. He was already sick. Malaria, I think. We were trying to make it home. I think he had internal bleeding. Or his heart just gave out." He brushed mud off the cuffs of his pants. "Dug a grave with a fucking trowel in the middle of nowhere. He was my friend."

Six looked at Geoff, then back at the Opt Out. Nobody said anything.

"You can go see for yourself," the Opt Out said. "Grave's right over there. I put his hat on the trowel. As if that'll last."

The sun streamed down on them and the air was hot and damp. The pain was back in Geoff's head and he squeezed his eyes shut. "If you lads don't mind," the Opt Out said, "I'll just walk along with you, if that's okay."

"No," Geoff said. "Sorry. We don't know you."

He nodded, like it was the answer he expected. "There's supposed to be trouble at the Marien River bridge," he said. "Gangs or something. Looting. That's what I've heard. There's more safety in numbers."

"No. Sorry."

"Well, fuck you too," the Opt Out said, without particular malice.

Geoff started walking and the others followed him. Six looked back at the Opt Out. He was using the tail of his shirt to wipe down his rifle. They walked for five minutes before Six spoke.

"Why couldn't he come with us?"

"I don't trust him. You don't just bury somebody. This isn't the movies."

"What's he supposed to do out here, call an ambulance?" Six said.

"I don't know," Geoff admitted. "I don't know."

They ate the last of the MREs in the late afternoon. Ahead of them, breaking the vista of flat soybean fields, lay a perpendicular strip of jungle, hiding the Marien River. The sun began to set behind them as they approached the line of trees. Cool mist blanketed the ground as the road ahead of them disappeared into shade. A shooting star, its smoke trail visible in the fading light, streaked overhead, followed by two more.

"It's such a nice evening," Six said.

***

His vision began to go dark, and all sound blurred into a deep, vibrating hum. He could see only a single point of light, and couldn't feel anything. He didn't know if he still had hold of his rifle. There was just the spot of light and the hum; no other physical sensations. He was floating, zero gravity, no pressure, no up or down.

Was I shot? he wondered. An unseen sniper in the jungle?

The white spot of light faded, blinked, held, and then flickered out. What was left had no form nor mass, and despite the absence of light, it was not dark. It was only his consciousness, no physical body. Stripped of his senses, he was alone in a void. He wasn't scared. He didn't know how to feel.

He thought of Elena, on her farm, without him. Elena getting the news that he was dead. Elena grieving, and then Elena getting over that grief, and moving on with her life.

This is it. This is it. This is it. He kept repeating the thought, but the volume of his own thoughts faded, becoming too faint to hear. The shark man was at his side. Well, okay. He'd kind of thought that's what the shark man was for.

Then his thoughts stopped, and the hum stopped, too, and it was just as it had been in the long, long time before he had been born.

***

A riverside boathouse of the old United Fruit Company stands on crumbling piers just a few feet above a wide, tumbling river. It is weathered and rotting and lists to one side, a square, two-story structure of plywood over a rusted steel frame with corner welds like gnarled knuckles. A narrow walkway with no guard rail runs along three sides; on this stands the tall man, looking down into the water.

"There it is!" he says, pointing.

He kneels down on the warped planks and points again, his finger almost touching the water.

"Ten feet, pretty big for a bull shark. Probably came upriver because of the storm. Yes, there." He points at a shadow in the water. "Is it? It could just be the clouds." He looks up at the sky, then back at the water. "No. It's a shark." He laughs. "That thing would eat you, you better believe it!"

Then he murmurs, "You can't believe how beautiful it is."

There is nobody else there. The boathouse creaks and groans in the wind. He stands and wipes sweat from his face, then kneels again and looks into the water.

The dark shadow in the river twists and turns in watery arabesques, as if it is performing a dance, just for him.

***

Hi Geoff,

Did you know I saw you as an old man today? Walking the streets, there was a very old man, maybe eighty, but still tall, still walking with energy, and he looked just like you. Or how you will look one day. Silver hair, still thick and wavy though. Wrinkles, yes, but still handsome. You walked past children playing soccer and you made a little move like you were going to join their game, and you laughed, and they laughed, and they smiled at you as you walked away into your great life.

Just thought you'd want to know that.

Stay safe,
Elena

***

Then it all rushed back to him—pain, heat, fear, and blinding light, starting as it ended with a little spot, but now in reverse, growing quickly until it filled his vision. He shielded his eyes—marveling for a moment at the awareness once again of his body—and Six gently slapped at both his cheeks. He was saying something.

"That's it, that's it, that's it, that's it," Six was repeating.

He was lying on his back on the road in front of the bridge. His arms and legs—everything worked. He sat up.

"What happened?"

"You passed out."

He put a hand to his right ear. It was bloody, and he was aware that his chronic and general headache had been replaced by throbbing pain on the right side of his head.

"Yeah," Emma said. "You smacked your noggin pretty good. Pretty dramatic if you ask me."

He started to stand, and Logan put out a hand to help him. Geoff wobbled for a moment but regained his balance.

"I'm okay."

They crossed the Marien Bridge and the little strip of jungle on the other side and were soon in open fields again, the air cooler with the fall of night, the sky clear and running fast with stars. Despite the beauty of the night, they were muted. The dog picked up on the mood and did not run ahead or attempt to play, but only walked alongside them. Six thought they would bed down, but Geoff just kept slowly walking. It seemed to them that the night was endless, full of nothing but the flat road and stars riding low in the sky. Geoff had an abiding sensation that the road had risen far into space, and they were walking along a corridor in the firmament. There was rain, briefly, from a single cloud that scudded across their path. Nothing else broke the crawling of hours. Time contracted with the cooling air, crawling from minute to minute with unsustainable effort. When at last light began to blush on the horizon, they had arrived at a village. It was immaculate, sparkling modern houses with tended green lawns and landscaping, but was crowded with residents of New Middlesborough who had fled the Opt Outs. Storm floods had not fully drained. Families slept right in the street, where the crown of the road lifted it above standing water. Geoff stepped over and around them. A young boy lying with his hands behind his head sat up to wave. Six carried the dog above the turbid waters.

Geoff's bruised head continued to throb, and he put a hand to his forehead. He felt his skull squirm under his touch, felt his teeth twist and loosen in his jaws, as if preparing to escape. The rising sun was blotted out by a fierce wall of black cloud that stole across the land. The first winds stirred the branches and swirled rubbish through the streets. Fingers of lightning spread above the trees, the light from the flashes lingering in the saturated clouds, lending them a hologram glow. Rain spattered into the village, and a nearby lightning strike sent everyone for cover.

"I'm definitely not tired of storms," Six said. "More. More storms please."

Geoff, Logan, Emma, and Six sheltered inside a decrepit concrete bunkhouse that a local boy told them had once belonged to an American fruit company. They shared it with a half-dozen refugee families. The windows were boarded over and the air was viscous and wet. A family started a small fire. Smoke filled the cramped space before the fire burned out, leaving only dark and the sound of the storm.

Six tried his phone again, and again got only the "Searching for Satellites" message. The dog paced uneasily at his feet. Logan leaned against a wall, dropped his chin to his chest, and slept.

Geoff lifted his head when the pitch of the wind rose or lightning struck nearby. Somebody arrived with a radio, but the batteries were weak and it worked for only a few minutes. They learned the winds exceeded ninety miles per hour, with gusts much higher. "It is expected to pass through in the next six hours," the voice on the radio said. Geoff was by now so thoroughly wracked with pain that he felt himself starting to slip into a hallucinatory fog. But he couldn't afford to lose his senses, even for the relief it might bring.

He reached out a hand and touched Six on the shoulder. "Tell me what happened back there at the bridge."

"You fell and hit your head and were knocked out."

"Why did I fall?"

Six looked at him and seemed to have decided something. "I'm pretty sure you have malaria, mate. Untreated malaria."

The rain stopped and the wind began rattling the plywood covering the windows.

"I think it's coming now," Six said.

"We'll be okay."

"God willing."

"You said there was no God."

"It's just an expression," Six said.

Geoff tried to massage the pain out of his temples. Rain came again and as quickly ended. The gusts leveled out into a steady howl.

"What was it like when you were knocked out?" Six asked. "Did you dream?"

"I thought I was dead," Geoff said. "I felt like I was leaving my body. And all I saw was light."

"What else?"

"I couldn't see or hear anything after awhile. There just wasn't anything."

Six sighed. "Yeah, that sounds like death."

"You know what death is like?"

"I'm starting to get an idea," Six said.

A child started crying in the dark building. His mother tried to soothe him. The air inside was misty, atomized rain driven through cracks and gaps in the crumbling structure. Geoff began to shiver.

"I don't think it was death," Geoff said, hugging himself against the cold.

"Obviously," Six said. "You're still alive."

"Right, but...maybe I was closer to not being alive, in that moment."

"Oh shit," Six said. "The dog." He stood up. "Where did he go?"

"He'll be fine."

"You always say that at first. And then later it all goes to shit." He searched the space, but the dog was gone. Six leapt to his feet and ran around the huddled families, asking each if they'd seen his dog.

Geoff sat in the dark, trembling with pain. He hugged himself and buried his head in his chest, but within minutes his chill turned to fever and he rolled onto his back and ineffectually fumbled to open his shirt. His breath came in ragged gasps, and he felt as if his heart was at war with itself.

"Relax. Relax and breathe."

He tried to answer her, but still could only gasp for breath.

"Just breathe."

He struggled to ease the muscles in his rib cage and neck, to relax his bulging eyes.

"That's it."

She closed his shirt across his chest and buttoned it.

"Thanks," he said, hoarsely.

She smiled and brushed his sweaty hair back. "You need to cut this," she said.

"I think I might have died. For a little while. Then I came back. There was a light. I thought it was Heaven."

"Maybe it was."

He shook his head. "I'm almost ready to come home."

"So then come home."

"I'm almost ready," he said.

He reached up for her. She was still there but farther away, just out of reach, her image wavering in the dark mist. Pain swept back over him and he rolled onto one side, both arms covering his head. He tried to talk but couldn't. His chest constricted and it took all he could do to continue to breathe.

Outside, the storm slashed and tore at the earth. The already swollen rivers began to spill their banks, carrying away great wedges of land. Trees weakened by the first storm snapped and fell, tumbled and rolled across the flooded ground. Some didn't break but were pulled up by their roots, without dispute. Others bent and remained standing. The building groaned as the storm, howling now, seemed to be trying to force its way inside. Geoff felt as if he could feel the building shifting, like an extension of his body, its stones and mortar grinding painfully, like broken molars.

A voice came from his side. The man in the suit, the shark man. "Close call back there," he said. "Very close call."

The storm whistled and screeched even louder, and part of the roof began peeling back. The loose tin banged and rattled in the wind, and rain slanted in, pelting the far inside wall. The families moved toward the dry end. Six was sitting next to him, huddled over.

"Where were you?" Geoff asked.

He opened his coat. Curled inside, sleeping, was the little dog.

***

Freshly strewn with mud and broken trees, the road they followed led them back into primary jungle, where it turned to just a path, and soon not even that. Six's phone had, for mere seconds, picked up satellites and displayed their location on a map. They had not recognized where they were, and then the satellites were lost again, and the map went with them.

In jungle again, green and chaotic with storm damage, they settled back into walking. The only plan was to keep moving west. They entered and kept walking through a small village where everyone was openly hostile. An old woman shouted at them, dogs barked and bared yellow teeth, forcing Six to scoop up his puppy, and shirtless teenagers glared.

"We look like all the other Opt Outs," Geoff said.

At the village outskirts, they found a crowd gathered around a boy who had glass bottles bound to his forearms and calves. He danced, twisted, leapt, and tumbled acrobatically, clacking the bottles together in time to the clapping of the watching crowd. Geoff had never seen anything so startlingly athletic and graceful. But the crowd noticed them and began to mutter threats.

"Don't say anything," Geoff whispered to Logan. They began moving away. Above them, a pair of shooting stars, one after the other, fired through the evening sky.

***

"It must be broken," Six said, looking at his phone again displaying the "Searching for Satellites" message.

"Maybe it has something to do with the storms" Geoff said. "Two hurricanes, one after another."

"A hurricane can't knock out a satellite way up in space."

"No, but it could damage the stations that communicate with them. Or knock down the towers. I don't know. But it's probably all related."

They were still in jungle, their pace slower than ever. The dog, impatient, had run ahead of them and had not returned, despite a distraught Six yelling his lungs raw. He continued to whistle for it periodically. Again they were plagued by hunger, by thirst, by blisters. Geoff's fever had not broken, nor had his headache eased. His vision periodically blurred, and when it did, he had to stop and shake his head to clear it.

They entered another village, this one completely deserted. They passed an overgrown soccer field and a few dozen clapboard cottages. The first few they searched had already been extensively ransacked, as had a small corner shop, but there they found a few cans of generic soda and some snack cakes in plastic wrapping. The sugar rush helped tame Geoff's headache and boosted their mood, although Six remained upset about the dog.

"We'll have to bed down soon," Geoff said.

"Why was that village deserted, do you think?" Six asked.

Geoff didn't answer.

Shortly before sunset, they entered what they thought was an even more derelict village. A faintly worn path led through stone columns into a grassy courtyard flanked by large buildings overgrown with vegetation. The trees were intact and formed a nearly solid canopy. Vines and bromeliads sprouted from the branches. A thin column of light-blue smoke rose from behind one of the temples, and as they approached, a Mayan girl of about twelve appeared in front of them. She didn't smile but waved, and then ran back behind the structure, from where, a moment later, a tall, middle-aged woman emerged.

"Who are you?" Six asked.

"Well, I live here," she said evenly. "So I think you should tell me who you are first."

"We're just passing through," Six said. "You didn't see a dog, did you?"

"I'm sorry, no," she said, but the question seemed to satisfy her. "I'm Gayle," she said. "This is the Anh Pac Archaeology Site. I discovered it."

***

Gayle had stocks of food—boxes and boxes of rice, beans, peanut butter, dehydrated milk, applesauce, freeze-dried chicken, and crackers, along with mounds of fresh produce: her camp kitchen overflowed with bananas, mangoes, spinach, and squash. She had a small medical kit, and with it she cleaned, disinfected, and dressed Six's wounded arm. Geoff accepted aspirin, but didn't mention his suspected malaria.

The girl sat with them, not paying attention to the conversation. She had black hair, cut bowl-style, and wore cutoff shorts and a Spiderman t-shirt. She hummed to herself and seemed impatient, and finally interrupted:

"Are you going to tell them about The Thistle Prince?"

"You can," Gayle said. "Later."

The girl shrugged and jumped up from the table.

Gayle took them on a short tour of the complex. "This was not a residential city," she said. "Most people lived on farms outside the complex. It was a civic ceremonial center. Holidays were celebrated here, important weddings, state political rallies, that sort of thing."

She flashed her powerful spotlight into the trees lining the courtyard.

"How old is it?" Logan asked.

"I think it was first constructed around six hundred A.D."

"I can't do that math."

"It's about twenty-six hundred years old."

Geoff lagged a little behind, fatigue washing over him.

At the rear of the complex, a lagoon opened a hole in the jungle. Gayle steered them away from it. "There's a big crocodile in there."

Gayle walked them over to the main temple, a pyramid with steps cut into all four sides, rising two hundred feet above the courtyard floor. A series of carvings, four feet high, ran across its base. "These glyphs tell the usual stories," she said. "Creation, birth of man, various gods, etcetera."

"What is The Thistle Prince?" Six asked.

"Oh, I'll let Juhan tell you about that. I expect she's itching to."

Gayle told them they could sleep in one of the small, hastily constructed cabins once she cleared out space, but she either forgot or changed her mind, because after the brief tour, she bid them good night, went inside her own cabin, and didn't come out again.

Juhan sat with them on a bench and watched the moon bob in the breeze above the trees and temples. The night wind blew steadily, keeping them free from mosquitoes and masking the jungle insect chorus.

"Where are you going to sleep?" Juhan asked them.

"In the grass, on the ground. Doesn't matter."

Juhan's eyes widened slightly. "You can't sleep out here," she said. "There are empty spaces at the back of some of the small temples. There are no doors, but you can drag some bushes or something across the front. I'll show you."

"We're used to bush sleeping," Geoff said.

Juhan hopped off the bench, shaking her head. "It's different here."

***

Geoff had slept erratically, and was awake when the canopy and temples began to glow a faint green. He walked into the courtyard, the grass and air wet, and to the main pyramid, where Gayle stood in front of a carved surface, the source of the green glow.

"It's a slow-burning phosphorus mix," Gayle said, turning as Geoff approached. "Burns off the fungus but doesn't harm the stone."

The phosphorus burned unevenly, flaring in small, bright volcanoes in spots, flickering to dark in others. It hissed as it burned. Geoff felt its heat on his face.

"What's under it?"

"That's the question. I have to burn off the fungus. I spent a week cutting off vines."

"Does Juhan help you?"

"She does," Gayle said. "She's actually been pretty invaluable."

Gayle flashed her light into the trees sporadically.

"It's all one living organism," Gayle said. "The fungus. It's like a carpet over the entire site. Probably two thousand years old, at least. Burning this little bit won't hurt it." She waved a hand at the glowing phosphorus.

"Do many people come out here?"

"Just some people from Juhan's town. I pay them to get my food, though I don't know for how much longer. You and your friends are the first to come out here in months."

Something crunched in the underbrush of the forest. Gayle flashed her light into the trees again.

"What is The Thistle Prince?"

"Oh, that. It's a jaguar. A legendary one."

"I thought there were no more jaguars?"

"There's at least one. We see his tracks and his kills. And sometimes we hear him in the night. It's a legend, but also very real."

The phosphorus hissed and popped. Geoff thought about the vision of the jungle cat in hiding he'd seen when atop the ferris wheel.

"How long will this take?"

"A day or two."

"What if it rains?"

"You can't put out burning phosphorus."

They stood watching the phosphorus until the first blush of morning began to play about the edges of the sky. In the opening of the canopy, high clouds caught the first rays, and soon they saw the red sun itself through the thick trees.

"Thank God for that," Gayle said.

***

While the temple face glowed and burned, they helped Gayle strip a smaller structure of its vine shrouding, hacking away at the biomass with machetes and piling the detritus to one side. "Astronomical observatory," Gayle said, after they'd cleared it. "These strips here"—she pointed to narrow, vertical gaps in the stone—"tracked the sun and helped people to know when to plant, when to harvest, that kind of thing. Based on what part of the wall the sun lit up on the inside."

Juhan arrived late-morning and helped carry away the cut vines. The day was again hot and sticky. Black clouds circulated above the canopy opening. Gayle fed them again, and they began preparing to leave.

Gayle had a generator and small power bank. Six plugged his phone into it and got the familiar error message.

"From what Juhan was saying," Gayle said, "the water still hasn't gone down."

"We have to go," Geoff said. "We don't have a choice."

They thanked Gayle and started out, but before they were a mile from the ruins, they found the bridge over the New Tyne River washed away, and the river itself swollen, running brown and fast and heavy with debris. They looked at it without speaking, then turned around.

***

There is risk to the hunt, danger in every conflict. This is just as true for the hunter as the prey. The tall man knows a constant feeling of tension, a fullness in his chest like something alive inside is trying to claw out of him. He is incapable of rest or stillness; he is like a shark at the bottom of a dark lagoon, circling constantly, waiting with inhuman patience. If he stops, he dies. He doesn't know what this feeling is. Most people would recognize it as the embryonic genesis of fear.

***

He fell into a darkness so total and complete that he eventually stopped blinking and straining and just closed his eyes again. It was the darkness of a tomb; the darkness of a place that had never before been stained by light.

It was silent. He couldn't hear even his own breathing. There were no pressure points on his body, and he couldn't orient himself. He didn't know if he was standing, sitting, lying down, or floating. There was only darkness and silence, and another presence trying to get in. A memory.

Just as a taste or a smell can trigger a memory and sweep you back to a forgotten time, all of it—the darkness, the silence, and the strange floating/not floating sensation—took him back, but he didn't know where to. He just knew an overwhelming sense of having done *this*—whatever it was—before. He also sensed he wasn't alone.

"I've been here," he said.

"We all start somewhere," a calm voice answered. "And we all finish somewhere. If time is a circle, then all things converge in the end."

"What if time isn't a circle?"

"Then it's a river, flowing in one direction only."

"So which is it?"

"It's not my job to know that."

There were other voices droning in the background, automated and robotic. *Flight six-five-five now departing. Now de-*

parting. Reset one, two, three. Flight six-five-five now departing. Reset, one, two, three.

He felt a great squeeze of pressure, and with it came other sensations: warmth, noise, and light, suddenly pouring down all around him like a waterfall. He came to feel his body again, hands and arms and eyes blinking back against the streaming light that grew stronger and brighter as it splashed around him.

Reset one, two, three. Flight six-five-five now departing. Now departing. Flight six-five-five. Now departing. Reset, one, two, three.

"How many times?" he asked. "How many times am I going to die?"

But he was alone again, and awake, and alive.

***

This is Sister Susie with Dirt Tiger Radio. We do not know why the radio waves are bouncing back to us. We do not know why satellites are falling. We do not know why we've had another hurricane. The government will pretend to know, and tell you not to worry. Be careful out there, citizens. We can see more storm clouds coming. This is Sister Susie with Dirt Tiger Radio.

***

He blinked. He was inside Gayle's cabin, lying in a cot. Six and Juhan stood over him too. A fierce rain hammered on the cabin. His head pounded. He put his hands to his temples.

"You have malaria," Gayle said. "It's very advanced. You've probably had it for weeks."

"You're not a doctor," Geoff croaked.

"I am, actually. Of archeology."

"You're lucky to be alive," Six said, leaning over him.

"You have to rest," Gayle said. Geoff stared straight up at the roof of the cabin, watching it pucker from the assault of rain above. Juhan and Six leaned further over him. Gayle crossed her arms.

"Do you have chloroquine?" Geoff asked.

"I'm afraid not."

"Then what good is rest?"

He sat up slowly. His head spun and he slumped back down on the cot. Gayle patted him on the shoulder and walked out of the cabin. Juhan followed him.

Six came closer. The rain stopped. They sat and listened to fat drops pattering into the roof.

"The Thistle Prince," Six said. "It's real."

"The what?"

"The jaguar. I saw the paw prints."

Geoff shifted on the cot, trying to take the pain out of his back. He closed his eyes. "There aren't any more jaguars."

"There's at least one. Juhan said it chased a girl from her town last night. They want us to kill it."

He opened his eyes and looked at Six, then closed them again.

"It's only a tiny little village. They're scared."

"Where's Logan? And Emma?"

"They went ahead to try to find chloroquine."

"They're not going to," Geoff said. He stood up, wobbled, waved Six away when he stepped toward him, and found his balance. He stretched his arms above his head and arched his back. Juhan walked into the cabin and addressed Six while pointing at Geoff. "Is he going to do it?"

***

Juhan stood silently while Six flexed and twisted his arm, trying to work a little more slack in the tight bandages, and Geoff lay sleeping. Finally, she said, "I can help."

"Help with what?" Six asked.

"The jaguar. I know where he lives. I'll take you there."

"First things first," Six said. "My friend has to get better."

Juhan shrugged. "You're gonna have to do it sooner or later."

"Really? Why's that?"

"It's not a normal jaguar, man."

"What's that got to do with us?"

"It knows you're here."

"But why—"

"I'm just saying," Juhan said. "It's not normal."

***

Juhan found tracks near the temples. Following them, she found they wound across the courtyard and came within twenty feet of the cabins. At night, they heard it cough and growl in the jungle. They heard birds go silent as it moved through the trees. Juhan brought stories from her village of the jaguar chasing a man into his neighbor's car, which was thankfully unlocked; of killing a goat; of standing on its hind legs to peer into the window of a house, and then sleeping on its porch.

"You have to kill it," she told them. "Nobody else can do it."

"Why not?"

"Because it's not a normal jaguar, man. I've been telling you. That jaguar's been shot ten times. He's still not dead."

Six looked over at Geoff, sleeping through his fever.

"Then what makes you think we could kill it?" Six asked.

"You got better guns. Army guns."

"We're not army."

"Same difference."

"Isn't it illegal to shoot a jaguar?"

Gayle, overhearing them, said, "There's not a lot of governance or law enforcement in the Big West. But then there's the moral question."

Juhan rolled her eyes. "People won't be worrying about morals when this thing is eating your face."

***

Gayle worked on the temple face, with Six assisting, handing her tools or helping brace the scaffolding. Geoff rose and watched from the doorway of the cabin, and went for short, shaky walks every few hours. In the afternoon, Gayle retreated to her cabin, and Six took a nap in the shady grass. Juhan juggled an old, half-deflated soccer ball.

"You play?" Geoff asked her.

"Not anymore. Too political."

"What does that mean?"

"I was top scorer two years in a row, but the coach's kid was on the team, and he put him in instead of me, just because he's a boy. You should have seen this kid. He couldn't run, couldn't pass, couldn't shoot." Juhan did a crude imitation and laughed. "We used to win every game. Soon as this kid started playing, we never won again."

"Never? Not a single game?"

"You know what I mean. We weren't as good."

"Yeah," Geoff said. "I played on some teams like that too."

"So you know, man," Juhan said gravely. "You know."

***

Geoff woke, sweaty and confused, but not in much pain, for a change. He stepped outside the cabin, taking care not to wake Six, and stretched his arms above his head. The night embraced him, warm like amniotic fluid. A few stars glimmered fuzzily through a thin blanket of cloud. Across the courtyard, he saw Gayle and Juhan silhouetted in the faint green glow of phosphorus. He crossed slowly to them.

"You figure out what this is?" he asked Gayle, pointing at the carving.

"It's an Ouroboros."

Cleared of soil and vegetation, the carving stood out in remarkable detail. Twenty feet in diameter, it showed an enormous serpent coiled back on itself, with its tail just about to enter its open mouth. Various faces and figures adorned the circular space defined by the snake. Juhan reached out a hand and lightly stroked the stone surface.

"It's the self-devouring snake," Gayle said. "We find it in the mythology of a lot of cultures. The Egyptians, the Greeks. And the Mayans, here."

"No snake would swallow its own tail," Juhan said.

"What does it mean?" Geoff asked Gayle.

"It's symbolic of unity, eternity. The circular nature of life." She drew a circle in the air with her index finger. "Look here." She pointed to the snake's gaping mouth. "Say we could run the film forward a few frames, and the tail goes into the mouth, and he starts swallowing. Where does it go?"

"His stomach," Juhan answered.

Gayle nodded. "Let's say a snake's stomach is long and thin, almost the entire inside of his body, which it's not, really, but imagine it is. The tail goes inside, and if the snake kept swallowing, what would it eventually run into?"

"The end of the stomach," Geoff said.

"And what is just beyond that?"

"The tip of his tail."

"But that's already inside his mouth," Gayle said.

Geoff processed this in silence. "It doesn't matter," Juhan insisted. "No snake would swallow its own tail."

Gayle looked at Geoff. "What matters is time. This moment, captured here, right before the tail enters the mouth—this is forever. This is eternity. Because once that tail goes into the mouth, the snake can no longer exist."

Flecks of glowing phosphorus fell from the carving. Geoff stared at the serpent, its head two feet long, elaborate lashes carved above its eye. He looked at the point of the tail, the small V shape it made, and imagined it going inside the snake's hollow body, coiling ever tighter, going deeper and approaching the inside of the tail. That's as far as he could imagine.

"I understand now," Juhan said. "Because it's a circle." She pointed at the snake and mimicked Gayle's circle with her index finger. "Circles just keep happening."

"That's right," Gayle said. She put her hands in her pockets and they all stared at the glowing carving.

Juhan looked up at Geoff. "You don't look good, man."

***

A small storm blew up in the morning, leaving everything in its wake soaked and steaming. Geoff ignored the pain in his spine and neck and walked stiffly after Gayle and Six, who were clearing vines from a small structure across the courtyard from the main temple. He helped from time to time, but often had to sit to calm his spinning head. Juhan came running up the jungle path. "It got her," he said. "It got her."

"Got who?"

"Cardena. Gerald's daughter. It got her last night."

"It killed her?" Geoff asked.

"Well no, she's going to be okay," Juhan said. "It slashed her leg and then a dog chased it away."

"It's scared of dogs? I thought it was an all-powerful magical jaguar."

Juhan scowled. "Are you going to help us or not? You have to wait for your other friends to come back anyway."

"I'm not killing a jaguar. But I'll put a few shots over its head if you think that might scare it away. And if you stop bothering me."

Juhan groaned. "Lame. But yeah. Better than nothing."

***

That night, Juhan claimed she heard its throaty purr and heavy padding as it stalked the wooden planks of the scaffolding Gayle had constructed. But when they shined a flashlight outside, they couldn't see anything.

Geoff floated between sleep and waking dreams all night, his malarial visions persisting. It was a clear night, and he watched stars glide above the trees, interspersed from time to time by shooting stars. One of them appeared to break up in the low atmosphere, each fragment leaving a trail of smoke. Starlight at times was so bright he had to shield his eyes; globular clusters and spiral galaxies flowed as Juhan softly sang to herself. He drifted in and out of sleep, waving a hand automatically at a cloud of tiny flies above his head. In a half-dream, an old woman came to him and said, "Come see." She took his hand and led him into the jungle, where the moon, the size of a car, sat among the trees. "This is where it rests," she said. He could see it expanding and contracting as it breathed. The old woman beckoned him to follow back out of the jungle. He looked over his shoulder and saw the moon slowly beginning to rise from the grass.

When the sun rose, they found a half-devoured peccary. They walked around it and looked into the jungle. "He's watching us," Juhan said. Geoff imagined it, low-slung like an Italian sports car, moving through tall grass, fresh blood on its muzzle, the damp earth vibrating with its raspy breath. It was meant to be here.

"We can make a trap," Juhan said. "I can gut a goat and we'll hang it from a tree. Dig a hole under it and cover it with branches."

"We don't have to gut a goat. We can use the rest of that thing." He pointed at the peccary.

"It would be better if we used a goat."

"Do you just want to kill a goat?"

"You don't understand. He's finished with that. He won't come back for it."

"A hole's not a good idea. One of us will just fall in it."

Juhan suggested a rope snare, and spent the day testing and practicing with it. Geoff had to lie down for most of the afternoon. Six continued helping Gayle around the temples. Another brief storm rolled through in late afternoon, and sunset was a hazy and unusually red affair. After dark, Juhan sat with Geoff, holding one end of the rope snare, the other end forty feet into the courtyard, surrounding the remains of the peccary.

"I'm gonna get out of here one day," Juhan said as they waited.

"How old are you?"

"Thirteen."

"There's no rush."

"Thirteen and a half," Juhan corrected herself.

"Where do you want to go?"

"It doesn't matter. Just away." She brushed hair from her forehead. "You married?"

"No. But I have a girlfriend."

"Where is she?"

"She's at home." Geoff looked at his watch. "I'm not staying out here all night," he said. "I need to sleep."

"Man, all you do all day is sleep."

"I have malaria."

"Everybody around here has had malaria."

"Is that why you want to leave?"

"What, malaria? No. It just sucks here," she said.

"What's so wrong with it?"

"We don't have anything. No wifi, no cell phone service. Only thing we got is a Dunkin' Donuts."

"You have a Dunkin' Donuts?"

"They had wifi there at first, but it broke, and they never fixed it."

Six came out and sat with them for a while, before going back inside to sleep. Geoff was fatigued but not sleepy. A fresh wind stirred the trees. They heard a bat fly close overhead.

"Why do you keep saying the jaguar is not normal?"

Juhan looked uncomfortable, and answered only after a long pause. "It's some old-time stuff. I don't believe it. But people say it's a spirit jaguar. Someone called it here as a curse against us. I don't believe that stuff," she hastened, brushing her hands together, as if divesting herself of the idea. "I know what you think about people out here, but we're not all like that. That's just what older people say. I like old people. But some of them talk some stupid shit."

"Who would have called it here?"

"An enemy. Maybe some guy, you know, going off with some other guy's wife, so he calls the jaguar for revenge."

Geoff went to sleep an hour later, with the rope snare, held by Juhan, still untouched.

***

National Weather Service
For Immediate Release

Failure of GeoSat Star-65 Weather Satellites

The National Weather Service is working in conjunction with the U.S. Air Force to determine the cause of the failure of all six operational GeoSat Star-65 weather satellites, which have been offline for over seventy-two hours. The total loss of data downlink suggests mechanical failure, with the suspected cause being faulty battery chargers which short-circuited, leading to a loss of orbital alignment and failure of the solar panels to adequately recharge the batteries. The failure of all six simultaneously suggests a celestial anomaly, such as unusual sunspot or solar storm activity, which may have caused the battery chargers to short-circuit.

The six satellites were launched sequentially in 2005 and 2006. Their expected life span is twenty years. Each is about the size of a school bus.

The National Weather Service continues to provide satellite weather data in partnership with the National Oceanic and At-

mospheric Administration (NOAA) and several international organizations whose satellites remain online for now. However, similar anomalies and satellite failures have been reported across multiple agencies. A new generation of weather satellites is being prepared for service, with expected launch dates early next year.

***

The town was exactly as he remembered, and though it had been three years, it seemed that not a single day had passed. There was his school. Behind it, he knew without seeing, was the rock-strewn soccer field, where he had once scored a goal in an important game, but then was later sent off, and his team lost.

There was his street, Melaleuca, named after the trees Spanish settlers had planted two centuries ago to soak up water and drain the swamps. As kids, they had peeled the papery bark and burned it under the sun with magnifying glasses. You could burn black lines in it if you moved the glass at just the correct speed, writing your name or dirty words, and the smoke smelled sweet, like roasted fruit. To smell it now would be childhood again.

There was his house. Small and square, unfashionable but sturdy, a lone and dusty cohune palm standing in the sun-lashed front yard. There, in the yard, was his father as he liked to remember him: broad shoulders, a neatly trimmed mustache, legs that were too short for his thick torso. He was powerful but not athletic, and at family gatherings or parties, he would run for comic effect, his stubby legs churning ineffectually as his massive torso wobbled above. "Here comes the bus!" he would shout, laughing.

He went inside. Wood paneling, Formica counters, an old refrigerator whirring rhythmically. School portraits of himself placed on a shelf. The TV. His father's chair. Down a short hall, he went inside the room he had shared with his brother. It looked the same: twin beds, some American sports posters—the Chicago Bulls—their shared desk.

He heard a voice in the hall, carefree and youthful. He had forgotten how young his mother had once been. Even at fifty, her face was mostly unlined, her hands free of spots, her hair still glossy and dark. She moved without pain. He watched her carry folded towels down the hall and into the bathroom, stepped aside to let her pass back to the living room. She responded to something his father said from outside with a laugh. Geoff reached out to touch her, but she had turned to his father, who had come inside.

They had grown up in England, his parents, and moved to Calem not long before he was born, when it was still a colony and such a move was a formality. Their life here had been a good one, but short. His mother and his father died within six months of each other. Father of a heart attack; mother, only an occasional smoker, from lung cancer. She had done chemo for two years but the cancer "had not responded the way we'd hoped it might," he remembered the English doctor saying. She got progressively weaker and sicker, staying alive for the sake of everyone else, until announcing she was done with chemo. She celebrated ending her treatment like some people might have celebrated paying off a mortgage or winning the lottery, and she passed, at peace and with no fear, three months later.

He watched them together, moving from the kitchen back to the living room, laughing about something. It didn't matter what. Then the edges of the room began to blur a little.

Not yet, he thought. I want to stay.

But the room began to fall away into a white haze.

***

Most days the tall man doesn't eat, and he never sleeps more than a few hours at night. He just walks. His GPS isn't working, but he knows his destination. Sometimes, a bus will arrive, and carry him for a few hours, the locals ignoring him. But a bus can't take him all the way.

The skies overhead in the daytime are hot and dead, increasingly hazy with particulates, or smoke, or the dust of meteorites. He can tell, even all the way out here, that there is no radio, no electricity, no planes vectoring through the sky. One afternoon, he stands on a gravel road, and he flips time and space in his mind, imagining that the blue sky above is the Pacific Ocean as seen by an astronaut looking down from orbit, the clouds below him instead of above. He wills away the grinding heat and humidity, and feels himself floating in the cold purity of space, and he wants to stay there.

He would not have to do his job if other people did theirs. That's why he is here. The government agency he contracts for was dissatisfied with the efforts to quell a left-wing uprising that, intelligence told them, was gaining favor with the masses. His briefings referred to "Marxists" and "insurgents." They always did. Here or wherever else he was sent to work.

He sees two workers in a field, and crosses rows of budding sweet potato to speak with them. They start at his approach; he sees their pockets are stuffed with potatoes, and he knows they are not workers, but raiders. He smiles at them, but they turn and run.

The next village is mostly deserted. A couple of dogs trail after him for a while. A man watches him from a shop as he walks past. "We have beer," the man calls. "Red Stripe, Bud, Labatt's. Got some aspirin. Matches, soda."

He keeps walking.

He shields his eyes against the sun. At a basketball court on the edge of the village, he watches four kids playing a game of two-on-two. The heat doesn't bother them. They run and jump and sweat through their shirts, ignoring him.

The road past the court disappears into fields and, near the horizon, karst hills and rainforest. Out there somewhere is a second road, he thinks, and a second walker, just like him.

He calls to the boys. "How far to the next town?"

But they just keep playing.

***

On the next night, Gayle and Six joined Geoff and Juhan as they sat by the rope snare. It had rained earlier, and after the skies cleared and the sun set, it became almost cool. It chilled Geoff's feverish skin, and soon he began to shiver, and had to drape his jacket over his bony shoulders.

"There's something wrong with the Moon," Juhan said.

She pointed at it, bedding down low to the horizon in a layer of thin cloud and mist which diffused its dim, yellow glimmer. The moon was oblong, like a rugby ball, but blunt on one end. "That's not right, is it?"

"It's the eclipse," Gayle said. "That's right. I completely forgot."

"How could you know?" Juhan complained. "No wifi."

Soon the eclipse moon sank beneath the horizon, the night darkened, bats spiraled above them, and they forgot about it.

"You think it will show up tonight?" Six asked.

"I don't know, man," Juhan said. "It's a mystery."

"Maybe we should have waited for him in your village," Six said. "That's where he seems to be all the time."

"My village is boring."

"Aside from the jaguar attacks, you mean."

They heard something moving in the bush. Gayle trained her flashlight on the trees as they edged slowly back toward the cabin. It went quiet again.

"Is it him?" Geoff whispered.

Juhan stared hard into the darkness. There was a rustling, and suddenly a shape burst from the trees and ran directly at them. Gayle tracked it with her light. Juhan leapt to her feet, but Six was already in front of her.

"You found me!" he said. He looked back at the rest of them and laughed, then clasped the little dog to his chest. "You found me!"

***

"Can you believe it," Six kept saying in the morning. "He found me. He found me! How could he do that? We've come all this way."

"We haven't come that far," Geoff said, lying in his cot with a hand over his face.

Six sat cross-legged on the floor, the dog in his lap and trying to lean back and lick his face. "What?"

"We just move slow. We haven't come that far."

"Anyway, the important thing is he's back!" He scratched the dog's neck, as it raised its chin to accommodate him.

"You should make a leash this time."

"He won't run away again."

"Because of the jaguar. And give it a goddamn name."

Gayle entered the cabin and asked for Six's help. As they started to leave, Geoff sat up in his cot, but a head rush sent his vision spinning. He lowered himself back down, and covered his face with his right hand.

"You okay? We'll be right back," Six said.

"The light hurts my eyes."

"Stay with him, Chirpy," he said to the dog. "I'll be right back."

Geoff moved his hand and looked at Six.

"You said to give him a name," Six said. "He's called Chirpy now."

"That's the worst name I've ever heard in my entire life."

"I'll give you a free pass today because of the malaria. You're not allowed to be this grumpy tomorrow."

Outside, Six followed Gayle to the Ouroboros carving on the main temple. She had a pile of metal pipes partially assembled into a skeletal structure. "It's scaffolding," she said, "but I can't finish it without some help. It shouldn't take long."

They worked through the morning, handicapped by some missing joint connectors and bolts. Gayle was able to fabricate makeshift replacements, but despite this, they had several false starts, and had to take apart sections they had already built and re-do them. Juhan came by, and Six sent her to sit with Geoff and play with the dog.

As they rested, the scaffolding now almost complete, Six said, "You said you discovered this site?"

"There were writings from a nineteenth century French explorer, René DeLille. The main structures he wrote about have all been explored. This was a footnote. I found it last March. You'd be surprised how many unexplored sites there still are."

"How does this work? I mean, who pays you to do this?"

"I work for an American university. Or, well, I did. To be honest, I'm not supposed to be here anymore. My grant ran out weeks ago."

They stood in front of the Ouroboros, and the newly constructed scaffolding. "This will help," Gayle said. "There are some symbols at the top. I think they're mathematical in nature."

"I'm terrible at maths," Six said.

Gayle crossed her arms in front of her chest. "So am I."

***

In the absence of treatment, malaria rarely gets better. Excessive bed rest only made Geoff more tired, a miserable insomniac's exhaustion that drained his will to exist. His head pounded constantly, and wretched cramps knotted his stomach. His skin took on a yellow pallor. Late in a sleepless night, he swung his feet to the floor and stood, groaning with effort. He shuffled painfully to the composting toilet.

On his way back, just before he reached the cabin, a small wind stirred the trees, and then stilled. The stillness felt like something more than a dying breeze; it felt like fear. The entire jungle seemed to freeze. The insect song stopped. The wind blew again, but the leaves remained silent, as if even the trees were scared. He had neglected to bring a flashlight, and in the immense dark could see only shadow and shades of black. But he knew what was there. Above his own thumping heartbeat and roaring blood, he could hear its raspy breath.

"Don't move," Six said softly from the cabin.

"Do you see it?" he whispered.

"I'm not sure. I see something. Just stay still."

He stood in the dark, imagining the jaguar circling him, coiled, about to pounce. It seemed the breathing, punctuated by a growl and cough now and then, came from all angles. But after a few minutes, there was a palpable release of tension. The jungle relaxed its grip, and Six said, "I think it's gone."

He felt his way back to the cabin. Inside, Six lit a lantern. Geoff dropped, exhausted, onto his cot. Despite the excitement, Six was soon asleep, leaving Geoff to his fatigue. His head spun and ached. Phantoms drifted in and out of his vision. Elena came and went, and with effort, he was able to bring her back again.

"You're still sick," she said.

"I want to leave. I'm not strong enough yet."

"You can't stay here," she insisted. "There are forces converging."

"What forces?"

But she was gone.

Geoff swung his feet to the floor and carefully stood. He waited until his equilibrium settled, then took a few steps to stand at the door. Outside, the courtyard was dark, framed by the even darker silhouette of trees above. But in the sky above the opening, a cascade of shooting stars fell from west to east. Geoff had a sense of depth; some of them were far away, others close. For a minute or two at a time, the sky would go still and dark, before another line of fire would bisect the night.

"What is it?" Six asked.

"I didn't know you were awake."

"Is it the jaguar again?"

"No. Look."

They stood together in silence, watching the light show.

Later, he found that he was standing atop a grassy hill cleared of trees, with views in every direction. Down at the bottom of the hill, two hooded figures stood with flashlights playing up into the sky. The flashlights revealed showers of stars, moons, planets, and comets with tails blown by solar winds. The wind rushed about his face, and the darkness all around him swallowed sound. Below, stars sparkled in the glow of the flashlights, and slowly spread above, until the sky was clotted with celestial phenomena. He had never seen anything so beautiful. So this is how it works, he marveled. This is where the stars live. Two strange figures spray the firmament across the heavens with flashlights. Why had nobody noticed before?

He woke, and then tried to fall sleep again, to force the same dream. But that never works.

***

The skies cleared at noon. Gayle worked at one of the temples all afternoon. Geoff sat in the sun. He waved off Six's protest and said, "It'll be good for me."

At three o'clock, the sky began to darken again. Black clouds swirled low. Everyone retreated to shelter. Lighting and hail tore into the trees.

"Damn," Juhan said quietly. "He was right."

"Who was?" Six asked.

"Gilmar. Old guy from my village. One of the ones always talking about spirits and ghosts and shit. He's been saying this jaguar coming around means it's the end times. He was right."

"It's not the end times," Six said. "It's just a storm."

"I know," Juhan said. "I was joking."

The storm blew itself out, and the skies cleared just before sunset. All that night, a fusillade of shooting stars fired across the sky, in all directions, leaving faint smoke trails in the still-wet sky, like scars across the shell of an aged sea turtle.

***

Dim light came from the window, and Geoff rose to it on unsteady legs. A glow came from behind the temples, and above, sparks and flashes crossed the night sky, like dandelion seeds of colored light. Elena would love this, he thought.

He fell back onto his bed and crossed his arms on his chest, and the full weight of his pain and longing collapsed on him. His chest heaved, and what he had suppressed so long he now let himself crave, and he lay there and mourned for not having Elena close, for not knowing if he would ever have her close again, and for suspecting he had ruined it long ago.

Outside, the sky was animated with light, sparks and streaks and wild palettes of oversaturated pinkrose nebula and fluorescence, shimmering quietly. Something of his pain and yearning abated. His breath slowed.

Something was coming. He couldn't know what; the jaguar, or Opt-Outs, or The Dirt Tigers, or something else. He didn't know what. But something.

Depot 655. He hadn't forgotten the mission. But something else was coming.

He relaxed his constricted chest, and again Elena came to him in thoughts sweet and narcotic, like a river of liquid holograms.

***

Juhan had gone back to her home before midnight, and returned to camp shortly after sunrise with an announcement: "Something fell from the sky last night."

"What was it?"

"What am I, a sky doctor? There was a big crash and now there's a big hole in the ground. Something fell."

"Where?"

"Right in the middle of town. I think it's a meteor. We've been having these meteor showers."

They all went. Geoff was tired but didn't feel any worse than normal. They reached the village after fifteen minutes, along a path through jungle that gradually thinned to overgrown fields. The village was more modern and orderly than Geoff expected, not blistered with decay or deserted like many of the villages they'd walked through in the Big West, with one main street and a dozen evenly spaced side streets crossing it. All the little clapboard houses on the side streets looked exactly the same, built from the same template, at the same time. People stood in front of the shops on the main street and watched them walk past. A group of teenage boys stood together, and one of them said something to Juhan as they passed, but she ignored it.

Near the far end of the town, just to the side of the main street, smoke rose from a crater in the earth. A few people stood close to it. Geoff peered through the smoke at the hole, about ten feet in diameter and half as deep. Road rubble, black and glazed from heat, lined the hole. But there was no object inside.

"What is it?" Geoff asked.

"Must have been a meteorite," Gayle said. "Blew itself apart on impact."

Juhan stepped lightly into the crater and began poking around. As soon as she did, a watching group of children followed her down.

"What's this?" Juhan said, holding up a twisted piece of metal. She reached up and handed it to Gayle.

"It's aluminum," Gayle said.

"Meteors aren't made of aluminum," Six said.

"There's more in there," Juhan said, reaching.

"Don't," Gayle said. "It's not safe."

***

The tall man stands in a dirt road, squinting against the sun at a column of dust rising in the distance. The road bisects a desiccated orange grove, leaves covered in dust hanging limply. He has already tried to eat an orange, but found it as hard and dry as a termite nest, and the sour sting of the peel only worsened his thirst.

Presently, the column of dust in the distance resolves into a dull blue pickup truck. The tall man stands in the center of the road long enough to force it to slow, then approaches when it idles. "Need a lift?" asks the driver, a middle-aged man.

"Yes, thank you." He climbs in and they start down the dirt road, the truck squeaking and groaning with every washboard bump.

"I'm going to Black Rock," the driver says.

"So am I."

They drive for an hour without a further word. At one point, the truck splutters and dies, but the driver, as if it is a common occurrence, simply opens the hood, bangs on the starter with a hammer, and the truck turns over without complaint. They ascend from the groves to foothills, green but storm-torn, and higher into the mountain range.

The tall man's migraine teases at the lining of his skull, but finally abates without erupting. He is left in a near-panicky state of surplus energy. He drums his fingertips on his kneecaps and rocks back and forth in his seat. Sweat soaks his hair and face. The driver sneaks a look at him.

"You feeling alright, mate?" he asks, breaking the long silence.

The tall man doesn't answer.

"I guess you got a good reason for wandering around the Big West by yourself." He looks over at the tall man.

"Birdwatcher," he says. This seems to satisfy the driver.

The tall man seems to snap to his senses suddenly. He looks at the driver as if seeing him for the first time. "Where are you going, anyway?"

"I'm picking up a refrigerator in Black Rock. Take it home, get it working, sell it on."

"Is that what you do? Fix things?"

"Fix them and sell them. If it's electric or has a motor, I can fix it."

"I like that," the tall man says.

"And you? Are you an American?"

"I am."

"Not a lot of Americans wandering around this way."

"They don't know what they're missing."

The driver holds his look for a moment and then laughs, and the tall man laughs with him.

They drive higher into the mountains. The sky clouds over, and a light rain falls. The road turns to mud, and the truck slides sideways a few times. Soon, they are moving at little more than walking pace. The driver hunches forward and keeps trying to clear the windshield with his sleeve, but only succeeds in smearing it further.

"When we were kids," the tall man says, "me and my best friend Jake bought a go-kart for twenty-five dollars. We had to rebuild the carburetor, and the first time we drove it, Jake broke the suspension. But it was an easy fix. We spent that whole summer racing that go-kart, trying to make it faster, trying to keep it running. "

The driver looks at him, then back at the road. "I remember go-karts," he says.

"One day, the go-kart wasn't there. I called Jake. He didn't have it. Someone stole it."

The driver waits for more. When it doesn't come, he says, "That's a shame."

The tall man feels his migraine building again. He feels sweat begin to bead once more on his forehead. His heart breaks from its metronome and begins to jump, to race, to trip over itself in its effort to combust. He feels words coming faster than his mouth can form them. With effort, he swallows them and they die. The tall man tries to control his breathing, his racing heart.

"How far to Black Rock?" he asks.

"Another hour, at this pace."

"I think I'll walk from here."

"Walk? What for? I'll get there faster."

"I have to get out."

"You don't want to be out there alone, mate."

He extends his right hand.

"I'm grateful," he manages to say.

The tall man's entire body trembles. A single drop of sweat falls from his forehead onto his rip-stop pants with an audible *thwop*. The driver looks at him with compassion. The tall man finally exits the truck and walks into the jungle, and as soon as the truck drives away and he is alone again, he feels his heart and nerves settle. He wonders why it always has to be this way with him, with people.

***

Juhan leaned against a tree overlooking the lagoon. A nagging wind rippled the black water, sending wavelets lapping into the muddy bank. The lagoon, football-shaped and a hundred feet across, was fed on one end and drained on the other by small creeks mostly hidden by jungle. On sunny mornings, Juhan knew, a large male crocodile stationed himself on the far bank and warmed his body. But this morning the sky was soft and gray, a smoky haze, and she scanned the water for the croc but couldn't find it.

A man appeared not far from the croc's sunbathing spot. Juhan had not heard him or suspected anyone was there. The man was looking directly at her. Juhan did not startle easily. She stared back, and a moment later, the man withdrew into the trees.

Juhan waited a few minutes before she went to the temple and told what she'd seen.

"Was he wearing a uniform?" Geoff asked her more than once.

"You're sure he was alone?" Gayle asked.

They waited all morning for the man, but he never came.

***

"It's been so long," Elena said. They walked down a footpath in a small riverside park in Wilshere. Grown men, clumsy and unathletic, played soccer on an AstroTurf field, sweating through their shirts. On benches lining the path, people, mostly old, sat and talked or read newspapers. A hot dog vendor leaned against his cart, a small flock of pigeons standing in front of him, as if awaiting a speech.

"I request leave every week," Geoff said. "They're not very good with paperwork."

"I know."

He took her hand, slightly sticky like his own in the humidity, and they passed two empty tennis courts and a playground. Ahead of them, he saw a couple playing happily with a dog. They soon intersected paths with the couple.

"Your dog is adorable," Elena said to the woman. "What kind is he?"

"He's a mix, some kind of mutt," the woman said.

"The best kind," Elena said.

They were a young couple, within a few years of the same ages as Elena and Geoff. The man had a consciously untrimmed beard and large, black-framed glasses, and the woman a colorful, hand-knitted hat. Geoff felt his neck prickle; he always assumed city people knew he was on leave from The Free State.

The dog, as if aware he was being discussed, began to turn in half circles, first one way and then the other. "He wants his toy," the man said, smiling. He pulled a small stuffed dinosaur from his backpack and tossed it to the dog, who caught it in his jaws and held it above his head, looking immensely pleased with himself.

"I almost got one," Elena said, leaning down and scratching the back of the dog's neck. "He's so sweet."

"Still could," Geoff said.

Elena looked up at him. "Who, me? Just me, alone?"

He wasn't sure how to answer that. Then he found himself looking down on the scene from above. He saw the stylish city couple with the cute dog, and he saw Elena practically glowing with happiness as she played with it. And he saw himself, trying to join in the simple joy of the moment, and being prevented by something. A shadow fell across his form. He marveled that the others couldn't see it; but the dog, ignoring him, did.

***

A fat moon turned slowly overhead and drew insects from torpor. In the lagoon behind the temple, ground mist fell across the water and scattered hazy light like a dusting of snow. The crocodile hung motionless, its bulk supported by the oily water. The frogs and birds and turtles of night knew from deep instinct that it was hunting, as still as it was, and that to stay alive, they must match that stillness.

Sensing a slight vibration in the water straight ahead—a small glass snake, perhaps—the crocodile sank beneath the surface and began tracking toward the disturbance. It pushed easily past tendrils of algae that grew up from the bottom, grasping for sunlight. In black water, in the black dead of night, the huge crocodile swam, and all the lake around it was silent.

***

Geoff steadied himself on the cabin's windowsill and tried to clear his head. He experienced cycles of lucidity lasting for a few minutes, interspersed with periods of his field of vision going snow white. He didn't know how long the whiteouts lasted. Sweat soaked his shirt. Six kept trying to talk to him. He saw something in the dark. A figure moving through the trees? He couldn't be sure. There it was, he thought, and there it was again. He tried to warn Six, but the words didn't come. He wasn't scared. He had known that what was out there was coming.

There, he definitely saw something. A man, hunched over, moving. Close to the lagoon. He could raise his rifle and fire a warning shot.

Who was he?

He looked behind him, but Six was asleep, and Elena wasn't there. He knew it wasn't real when she came to him, but it felt real, and he liked it. He liked it even though it only happened because he was sick.

I could die here, he thought. This time I really could.

He stared into the dark, but the man was gone.

***

A distant, throaty roar echoed around the forest, almost lost among the ambient insect chorus. Just enough moonlight came through the clouds for Geoff to see Six nod and point: across the lagoon. They rose from their hiding place in the ferns and began to silently trek through the bush, Geoff and Six side-by-side, Juhan just behind. Geoff brushed away an orb weaver spider's web, and steadied his quavering vision. Heat lightning flashed silently above them, briefly illuminating popcorn clouds towering above the valley. The roar came again, closer now, directly ahead. They slowed, placing each foot with precision, rifles cradled, and paused at the tree line. Beyond lay the lagoon, its surface disturbed by a faint breeze, glittering in the moonlight.

"He's close," Geoff whispered.

But almost as soon as he said it, the roar came again, this time impossibly far away, and almost directly behind them.

"I told you," Juhan said.

***

Juhan sat by as Geoff and Six cleaned their rifles. The dog sniffed aimlessly at the ground. Thunder had been billowing through the trees and the valley for hours, and the still, thick air began to stir.

"Maybe we should wait until the storm is gone," Six said.

Geoff glanced at the sky, then turned back to his rifle.

"There's always another storm, man," Juhan said.

***

Shapes blurred to shadows, the daytime palette only gray and white and black, the air now permanently soaked with a thin haze of smoke. The stars blazed down at him and illuminated the jungle in pale blue. At night, he walked the bush with Six, following the growls and coughs and roars which came from everywhere but led to nothing. All they wanted was to get close enough to see it, to fire shots above it and maybe scare it away permanently. But they had not yet got close enough.

His illness manifested in waves, some days his energy and appetite almost normal, others his fever peaking in a miserable fog of pain and congestion, his ears stopped up as if with mud, his sinuses filled with cement. He felt a constant sense of movement, not a spinning or whirling, but a shifting from side to side. It was difficult to focus on anything. Whatever he tried to look at, his eyes just slid on past, refusing to stop.

When he was with Six and the jaguar was near, the shadows took no form but remained shadows. There was no Elena, no shark man, no voices. They sat inches apart in the bush for hours, a part of the bush themselves, centipedes and tarantulas scurrying across them on their way to somewhere else. He shifted his feet slightly to prevent vines from permanently entangling him. There were times the raspy breathing was so close he swore he could feel its warmth on his neck; but there was nothing to shoot at, and minutes later, the growl would come from far away, across the lagoon, above the valley.

In the dark, he could see Six's face, stony with concentration.

"I'm worried," Six said.

"It's okay. We'll scare him off."

"It's not that."

Six pulled his phone from his pocket but did not turn it on. He simply held it in his hand, turning it over a few times while inspecting it.

"There's something wrong with the satellites," he said.

Geoff looked toward the sky, covered in dark cloud. "They taught us to navigate without GPS," he said. "Even without a compass. Using the sun, the moon. Even an old watch. Do you remember that?"

"I didn't pay attention."

"Well, look at you now," Geoff said.

"Look at *you.*"

A small vortex of mosquitoes whined around them. Geoff slapped one on his cheek, then held up his fingertips to inspect it.

"That's great," Six said. "You're going to get 'extra malaria.'"

Geoff said, "I guess Logan and Emma aren't coming back?"

"Would you?"

They heard the roar, dry and raspy, close. He closed a fist and then pointed, and they rose and moved through the bush without as much as a snap of a twig. Despite their misgivings and regrets about joining the Free State, they'd become good at this. They whisked through tall grass and ghosted above the leafy forest floor like stingrays gliding above a reef. The roar came again, still closer, and Geoff thought this time there was something in it that said, Yes. I'm here.

They skirted the edge of the lagoon and paused, waiting. Across the water, the silhouettes of the temples loomed black against the milky night sky. Geoff took a step forward, squatted down, and patted the surface lightly with the palm of his hand, *pap pap pap.* Across the lagoon, a great dark shape drifted in the water. It turned and paused.

Pap pap pap. It was too dark to see. Creamy clouds reflected dully off the surface, the glimmer and shine broken by a v-shaped wake. It came closer. *Pap pap pap.*

"What are you doing?" Six whispered.

"I want it to come closer."

"The crocodile?"

"The jaguar. If it hears splashing—"

"There's a crocodile in this lagoon," Six said.

Geoff stopped patting the water for a moment, but then started again.

"Fuck this," Six said. "If you want to get yourself eaten, go ahead." He took a step back, but didn't leave. The water in the center of the lagoon swirled. A small fish jumped in alarm. Geoff felt blood roaring through his head, but he heard only his palm slapping the water. He pointed a finger in the darkness at the wake coming ever closer. "Mate," Six implored. But Geoff didn't stop. Six took another step back.

The v-shaped wake dissipated; whatever was carving it into the lagoon descended. Geoff finally stopped, but he didn't rise from his crouch. The spent wake lapped at the toes of his boots. He had come this far. He wanted to see what was behind it all.

"It's here," he said.

He slowly pulled his flashlight from a pocket and switched it on, but instead of shining it at the water, he turned and played its wide beam across the riverine jungle from which they had just walked. There, reflected in the flashlight, was a pair of large, glowing green eyes. Geoff tried to shrug his rifle off his shoulder while still holding the flashlight. The eyes stayed fixed on him. He could see the faintest outlines of its powerful form. Then, apparently without coiling or tensing in any way, the form vanished. Seconds later they heard it roar, in triumph, Geoff thought, and already far away.

***

Gayle climbed over the temples, taking notes and drawing sketches in her notebooks. Six played with the dog. Geoff was somewhat more aware of the fluctuations of his illness, of the spikes and troughs of fever and the coldbone body aches, and the ongoing tapestry of hallucinations, different people and shapes and voices coming in and out of his consciousness. Yet his senses snapped into total focus during his excursions into the jungle with Six.

The task took on more urgency by the day. It killed two goats, Juhan reported. It was seen in the center of the village, and then disappeared just as quickly. Six fashioned a leash and no longer let the dog outside without it.

They heard it every night, and went out to find it when Geoff felt up to it. They slid through the bush together with the silence of river eels. But the jaguar seemed to orbit around their movements, sometimes ahead of them, sometimes behind. Juhan came with them some nights, pointing out possible routes through the bush, offering suggestions, complaints, and ultimately withering criticism of their efforts.

"You guys still don't know," she said, shaking her head. "Still don't know about this thing."

One night when they were alone, having again followed tracks and sounds that led nowhere, Geoff, after a sudden wash of fatigue, said, "I'm tired."

"No shit," Six said. The bush around them pulsed with quiet life. They heard the distant sound of a car starting somewhere in Juhan's town. Six, sitting against a tree, picked up a small pebble, turned it in his hands, and inspected it in the dim ambient light of the moon.

"Wow," he said. "Oh, wow."

"What?" Geoff asked.

"Shit, mate. Oh, shit." He stood and rubbed his face with both hands. "Goddamn it."

"*What?*"

"I just remembered that letter about my student loans."

Geoff started to laugh but was interrupted. The roar came from the west. They listened for it again, and when it came, they began moving in unison.

"This way," Geoff whispered.

They moved into tall grass that tugged at Geoff's clothing. In a clearing, they paused to listen. The air was completely still, but symmetrical rows of clouds raced above them, driven by high, silent winds. Moonlight flickered around them as if projected through a zoetrope. The roar, when it came, was receding. It was getting away again. They raced after it, the grass growing taller. Soon, they had to push it aside at head height with their rifles.

But then it was there again, the roar, closer than before. Closer than ever. Through the grass to his left, from what seemed like no more than ten feet, Geoff heard a low growl, felt it in his feet.

"This is no good," he whispered.

He motioned to Six to spin around, and they brought their backs together, rifles at the ready. The top of the grass stirred at eye level. They turned, looking and listening.

A wet, throaty cough, followed by raspy breathing, came from all sides.

"This is not a good place to be," Six said.

"But this is where it is," Geoff said.

"Should we shoot now?" He half-pointed his rifle at the sky.

"It has to see us do it. It has to connect the sound with humans."

They began backtracking, slowly at first, before speeding to a light jog. The next roar came from ahead and slightly to the right; they weaved slightly left.

"Go, go, go," Geoff urged, possibly to himself, as they ducked and snaked through the grass. The next roar seemed infused with anger. It was close; it was coming. Geoff felt the ground tremble. Even the insects stopped chirping and screeching. Clouds rolled across the moon. He began seeing shapes in the grass. The jaguar's head, yellow eyes rising to meet his. A crocodile sliding off the bank and disappearing into the tall grass. Clouds and the moon.

He looked up. Red wingtip lights of a jet cruising in the high reaches of the atmosphere blinked through the clouds.

A plane. He hadn't seen a big plane in the sky in months.

They saw the clearing ahead, tall grass flattened as if by a flying saucer, or a hoax. They broke into a dead run. Now the roar became a howl, high-pitched and angling through the grass, directly at them. A strangled cry died in Geoff's dry throat. He spun wildly as he ran, his rifle raised in front of him. Something crashed through the grass to his right, coming right at him. He didn't want to kill a jaguar, but he raised his rifle.

They burst into the clearing and stopped.

The tall grass waved in their wake, then stilled. Rows of cloud rolled on, driven by high-altitude winds. Gradually, insect song came back to the jungle.

From far away, they heard a muted roar.

Juhan was waiting for them when they got back. They didn't have to tell her.

***

A single cumulonimbus cloud, bathed pale blue by a half-moon above, hung over the valley, its anvil rising to cover most of the jeweled sky. Lightning flashed from within its stacked column, the bolts occasionally springing from the cloud mass to stab downward at the jungle; but it was distant enough to evince only murmurs of thunder.

"Sometimes I look at the moon," Six said, "and I think, it's incredible that people have been up there. But then, on nights like tonight, when it looks so close, I think you could almost reach up and touch it. Pretty crazy, going to the moon."

Lightning flashed high in the anvil. Every few minutes, a shooting star crossed the sky, burning out or disappearing behind the cloud mass. The wind freshened and the air felt almost cool. The rainy season was ending.

Geoff shook his head to clear his vision. It was the first sign of a migraine. "We should go," he said. "I don't want to just sit here."

"We can't find it when we hear it," Six said. "We can't find it when we know it's standing fifty feet from us."

"We have to," Geoff said. "We still have something to do."

Thunder, low and rolling like a distant train, spread through the jungle around them. Cohune fronds rustled in the breeze. The half-moon rode the wind.

"Tell me you're not still thinking about that fucking mission," Six asked.

Geoff, sitting against a tree, rubbed his face and exhaled.

***

Geoff felt rested enough for an evening walk. He found Gayle kneeling in front of the Ouroboros carving, squinting at it, repeatedly bumping her right fist against her right knee.

He began to speak: "Figured it o—"

"Still a mystery," she interrupted.

***

Geoff woke. Juhan stood over him, out of breath and whispering. It was dark and his head hurt, and he couldn't understand what she was saying.

"What?" he groaned.

"It's outside," Juhan said. "It's outside right now. It chased me."

"Did you see it? Actually see it?"

"You never really see it," Juhan admitted. "But it's there."

She helped Geoff stand. They woke Six and told him what was happening. The little dog began to growl at the door. Geoff grabbed his rifle.

Six closed the dog in the cabin, and they stepped outside into the dark. He shined his flashlight around the courtyard and the trees. A breeze came from the direction of the lagoon. "That way," Juhan said. "We should stay upwind. We can circle back around if it's not out there."

They walked along a path skirting the lagoon. Geoff could not tell if the soft roar in his ears came from the tumbling water, or the jaguar, or from inside his own head. They rounded the lagoon and stepped into the dark forest. The trees closed above them. From everywhere, Geoff could hear a crackling growl. His head began pounding, and he couldn't see, couldn't focus. It was all shadow, a rich darkness without depth. They forced their way past the roots of a banyan tree and branches that grasped at their shoulders and tried to pull them back.

"It's there," Juhan whispered.

A dark shape crouched in a depression behind the tree. Geoff blinked, unsure of what he was seeing, unable to distinguish form from shadow. Juhan whispered something, but he couldn't hear her. Geoff took another step and raised his rifle. A torrent of sweat fell from his face. Juhan placed a hand on his shoulder and whispered, "You better be ready to shoot again if it doesn't scare."

In his hands, the rifle suddenly felt alien, like some kind of viral appendage that had grown onto him. He wanted to shake free from it and run. He didn't want to shoot. But then the dark shape stirred. It seemed to swell. Was it moving? Was it poised to jump? In the ambient light, he thought he could see the faintest outline. He whispered to Six: "Torch."

Six flicked on his flashlight. The batteries had weakened in their travels, but there it was, sitting upright, its head perched unmoving on muscular shoulders, staring back at them with white eyes.

"Now," Juhan hissed.

Although it sat in calm repose, Geoff had never seen anything so potentially powerful. It bristled with energy, like a living embodiment of the ion-bloated electrical storms that had plagued their weary travels. It locked eyes with Geoff and did not waver.

Now. Geoff aimed a few feet above its head and pulled the trigger. The rifle did not jam.

At first there was no sound, just a white flash. Then the report exploded in his pounding head as the channel in the air it had torn clapped back together. He staggered backward; Six caught him. Waves of pain came and his eyes watered.

The jaguar had not moved.

"Shoot it," Juhan urged.

"Bad idea," Six murmured.

The jaguar, still staring at them, slowly raised a paw and methodically licked it a few times.

"Please," Juhan said.

"This isn't going to work," Geoff said. He started slowly moving backward. "We're not supposed to be here," he added, cutting off Juhan's protest. "Let's go."

They backed into the path, into another warm rain. Geoff again heard the growling, the roar. They kept walking backward, Six keeping his flashlight on the trees, until they reached camp.

They found Gayle sitting with the dog in the cabin. She stood when they entered. "What was that shot?" she demanded.

"We got our shot," Six said. "But it didn't scare."

Geoff, shaking and exhausted, dropped into his cot. Juhan stood next to him, frowning.

"You let it go," she said. "You just let it go."

"We did what we said we'd do," Six insisted to Gayle.

"You'll feel different if it comes after you," Juhan said. "You'll feel different if it gets your dog."

They were silent for a minute. Then Gayle said, "Well, we'll know if it's still around soon enough." She said good night, and left for her cabin.

"We're not gonna get a better chance than that," Juhan said, sounding more resigned than disappointed.

Geoff rolled onto his side. "You were the one that kept saying it's not a normal jaguar. Well, you were right."

Juhan acknowledged this with a half-nod and then left them.

The wind soughed through the trees. Six stood and looked outside into the dark. A shooting star crossed the sky, then another.

"We can't do anything more here," Geoff said.

"What about Logan and Emma?"

"They're not com—"

"I know. What about the water?"

"We'll fucking swim if we have to."

Presently, they both slept. Geoff's sleep was again plagued by fever dreams. He woke with a groan, his head soaked. The cabin was still; no shadows, no visions. He stood with effort and opened the door. His head spinning, he searched the dark silhouettes of the temples, half expecting to see the jaguar. Thick clots of stars rode the wind that rustled the cohune palms. He leaned forward into the dark, into the breeze, and felt it carry steam from his forehead.

Had the others seen what he had seen in that moment of pure fear, in the dim glow of the torch, and in the white flash of the rifle? Maybe they had only seen a jaguar.

He had seen his life and his death, and all the possible variations of both. He had seen eternity reflected in the jaguar's eyes. He had seen The Thistle Prince, the convergence of all possible forces, all possible things, and he knew it would be here for a very long time, long after they were gone. And he knew, too, it was another failure, another missed chance to prove himself.

***

In the morning, they said goodbye, Six holding the dog to his chest, Geoff weaving slightly on his feet.

"Good luck," Gayle said. "Come back if the water is still high."

Juhan stared at them dully, arms crossed, drawing patterns in the sand with her big toe, and shaking her head theatrically.

"Thanks for trying," she said. "I'll miss you guys. I knew you wouldn't get him. But thanks for trying."

***

The walking was again hard. The jungle rapidly depleted the supply of food that Gayle had donated, so Geoff instituted strict rationing. They tried to sleep through a midnight downpour, but the rain eventually chilled them, and they staggered on through the night. In the morning, they were grateful for the sun at first, until it rose high and brought heat and steaming humidity. They cycled through walking and resting into the afternoon. The dog, always sprightly, alerted them to something ahead. They slowed, then crept through the understory, rifles raised. From ahead, they heard a scream, and another one, and then what Geoff was sure was laughter. Suddenly a shape burst through the jungle canopy above them, and a person went flying past in the air, dangling from a wire they had not seen.

They followed the line into a clearing, and found a half-dozen people standing atop a wooden platform thirty feet above them, strapped into harnesses and wearing safety helmets with cameras mounted on top. Four men—they all had beards—and two women, all of them young and fit. Tourists. Six started to speak, but Geoff put a hand to his face.

"Fucking awesome," one man said, in an American accent. "That was sweet!"

The group had a guide. "Ready to go again?" he asked.

"Let's do this shit!"

Six cradled the dog to his chest. He and Geoff backed slowly into the bush, and they waited until the tourists launched from the platform and flew into the canopy, hooting like gibbons.

Late that night, Geoff, in a hot, feverish sleep, jerked awake. His shoulders pinched with cramp. He stretched his arms above his head and yawned, rubbed the sleep from his eyes, then gave a start when he recognized a shape looming in front of him.

Standing over him was an insect, gangly and huge, taller than he was, bipedal like a human. Iridescent wings fluttered on its back. It curled its forelegs in front of its face like a mantis, and silently regarded Geoff with glittering, multifaceted eyes. It preened and made a soft gurgling noise, then slowly reached a long, hooked foreleg toward Geoff, who was too startled to move. The insect's foreleg hovered an inch from his face, then gently stroked his cheek with the smooth, round backside of a cold claw, and Geoff felt a surprising and profound sense of peace. A moment later, he fell back to sleep. When he woke before first light, he'd forgotten the insect, or the vision, but the sense of peace lingered.

***

This is Sister Susie with Dirt Tiger Radio. We know you probably can't hear us. We know satellites are still burning up in the sky. Citizens, stay safe out there. This is Sister Susie with Dirt Tiger Radio.

***

Rainwater pooled an inch deep atop the salt flats, reflecting a setting sun. They walked around the boundary, salt marl and mud caking their boots, Six carrying the dog through the muckiest patches. The sun settled atop the Salt Top mountain range, slowly rising to cover more of the sky, separating jungle from desert. Emergent stars began to shine down on them in the growing dark. The wind came across the pans with nothing to stop it, an unsettling low whistle which rose to a howl when it gusted, and Geoff felt a chill at his neck.

The border of the salt pan meandered, with branches and deltas of forest intruding into the flats. They crossed a narrow strip of forest, emerged back into the pans, and saw, in the distance, a shimmer of sprinkled fire lights, with figures moving in silhouette around them. Geoff reflexively reached for his binoculars, before recalling they'd been lost in the first hurricane.

"Let's go around," Geoff said.

They crossed back into the forest, intending to flank the village. The wind freshened, rustled the leaves, and then dropped; in the silence, the dog began to growl. Geoff motioned for them to stop.

He peered into the dark. A dim glow came through and around the immature tree trunks. A handful of rectangular shadows blocked the light. One of them shifted, then they were blinded by a flashlight in their faces. A woman's voice followed.

"What do you want?"

"Just to pass through," Geoff said.

"What are you doing out here?"

"We just want to pass."

The shadows stepped closer. Geoff could hear the metallic clanks and dings of weaponry being brandished.

"Free State doesn't come out here for no reason."

Geoff groaned slightly as his temples twitched in pain. He put up a hand to shield his face from the light. The woman flashed the light from Geoff to Six and back again. She stepped closer and moved her flashlight's beam to her own chest, displaying the Dirt Tiger tarantula symbol.

"Where's the rest of your squadron?" she asked.

"They took the Opt Out. Or deserted."

"Yeah," the woman said. "I hear there's been a lot of that."

Geoff's eyes adjusted to the flashlight. In its glow, he could see the people facing him. They were young, strong-looking men and women, brandishing their weapons casually but not inattentively.

"If you two are deserting, you're going the wrong way."

"We're looking for something," Geoff said.

She laughed softly. "There's nothing much out here but us. But if we're what you were looking for, I think you can see you're badly outnumbered."

Six patted Geoff on the shoulder and gave a slight tug, as if to pull him back. "What do you say, mate? I think she's right."

"We're not looking for a fight," Geoff said.

"Well now, that's funny. Because you willingly joined The Free State."

"Based on lies they told us," Six said. "I was supposed to have my student loans forgiven, but you should have seen the letter they sent me. With the accrued interest, it's actually worse now than—"

Geoff elbowed him in the side and he stopped speaking.

"This government," she said, "sacrificed the youths of an entire generation for this crusade to forcibly eliminate a legitimate political movement. We're just lucky you're so hopeless at it."

"We're not hopeless at it," Six said. "We just don't want to do it."

"What about you?" she said, turning to Geoff.

He was silent for a long time. "I have my own agenda," he said.

She squinted at them. "I know what you're looking for. You're not going to find it, but you can go that way, if you must," she said, nodding toward the salt pans. "If you come near our camp, I'll shoot you both myself."

***

Dear Geoff,

They say the solar storm is only going to get worse, and more satellites are going to fail. My mobile hasn't worked for more than a week. I'm guessing it's even worse for you. I have three 'undelivered' emails to you sitting in my outbox. But I'm writing this one to you anyway.

I saw Trinity Chadwick in the city today. I don't know if I ever told you about her. I've tried not to think of her over the years. We were friends in primary. We were always together with a group, but we didn't often do things alone, just the two of us. Still, we were friends. For a few years, at least. Then, I think in sixth grade, she started to put on weight, and her skin got bad. And one day—God, this is so hard to admit—I wrote her a note, and handed it to her in the hall as I was walking past her. I didn't even stop. I can't remember the exact way I worded it, but the note said something like this: 'Dear Trinity, we can't be friends anymore. I am sorry.'

Can you believe I did that?

Imagine this little girl, eleven or twelve years old, already probably wondering what was going on with her body, already hearing whispers about herself, maybe even her parents or brothers saying something about her weight, or her skin. And then I hand her that note. Can you imagine the hurt, the damage that has to do to someone that young? I don't know if you ever get over something like that.

But she forgave me. We weren't friends for a year or two, and then our paths just sort of naturally crossed again.

She was still big, but I guess I thought I was being all grown up and mature by going ahead and being friends with a fat person. The thing is, she had plenty of other friends. She didn't need me to do her a favour. But that's what I thought I was doing.

Every day, I kept expecting her to say something about the note. But she never did. Finally, one day we were at lunch with a few other girls, and we weren't really involved in the discussion, and I leaned toward her and whispered, 'You've never said anything about that note I gave you.'

She looked surprised and said, 'What note?' I started to explain, but she cut me off, laughing. 'Sixth grade? Oh God, Elena, who remembers anything from sixth grade? I'm sure it was nothing.'

Then she reached over and gave my arm a little squeeze, and gave me a kind look, and I understood. She remembered the note alright, but she forgave me. She moved away after high school and we didn't keep in touch. I still feel guilty. Part of me wishes she hadn't forgiven me so easily. But I hadn't thought of her in years, until today. It's funny how the past can come rushing back at you like that. You want to change it, but you can't. Anyway, it was great to see her, and we're going to get a drink next weekend.

The past is weird. It's the one place everyone has been, and the one place nobody is allowed to go back to.

Take care of yourself.
Elena

***

The salt pans were dry and the surface crunched under their feet like brittle jewels. Sounds rushed at them from the distant forest, short bursts of what Geoff thought was construction, pneumatic hammering or diesel machinery, but the night was dark and a salt fog hung low to the ground and they couldn't see much beyond their own feet. At one point they heard a mammalian howl, low and mournful, and the dog, tethered to Six by the makeshift leash, sat down and responded in kind.

The skies cleared. Blue light from stardrift above sparkled across the salt like bioluminescence. The moon in full rose above the mountains, but Geoff saw it as a different moon, larger and covered with the patterned lights of civilization. He pointed a finger at it and found it was within reach, and a spark of static electricity arced from his finger to the cool, cratered surface.

Another creature howled in the dark. The dog ignored it this time. Geoff's headache returned, and with it came a creeping, cold feeling in his veins. His breathing became more labored, and he felt a burn in his legs with each stride. They took a final step in salt and reached the shore of the pans, then began ascending the sloping foothills. They climbed a small crest, and through the trees ahead of them, in the rising shimmer of morning, they saw the first peak, the faintest dusting of snow embellishing its jagged angles. Blankets of cloud shrouded the peaks beyond. In between them, green forest rose and fell in a series of valleys and canyons.

"We have to be close," Geoff said.

They stood staring at the distant mountains, blurry in the smoke-haze sky, impossible to gauge how far away. The dog, impatient, began prancing in place.

"You wanted to come, so here we are," Six said. "But there's not going to be a reward for this."

Geoff sighed. The dog whined.

The three of them continued on.

***

The climb grew steeper. They were aided by a strong wind that pushed at them from behind, countering their fatigue. They rested on small plateaus and Geoff even managed a very short nap, ten minutes of fitful sleep that invigorated him for the final push. With altitude, tropical jungle began to give way to pine forest. Through the trees ahead of them they could see a massive silvery disk, rippling and reflective, like an enormous flying saucer that had crashed on its rim.

"What is that?" Six asked as they approached.

They heard the gentle lapping of water as they cleared the trees and emerged on the sandy shore of a lake whose surface tilted ahead and above them, climbing with the landscape.

"Tell me you see this," Geoff said.

"Yes," Six said. "It's the Sloping Lakes of the Big West."

The Sloping Lakes of the Big West, the water held in place by strong updrafts and gravity that worked just a little differently here. Just like the stories had said.

They leaned into the slope and walked along the shore, climbing with the water into thinner air.

***

In the higher reaches they began encountering quartz tumbler cloud bands which refracted the afternoon sun into rainbow chromoflares and left a fine mineral dusting on their clothes and skin. Each time they emerged from a cloud bank the trees were taller. Small streams feeding the Sloped Lakes below them made for easy drinking. They felt no need to rest. Geoff's headache abated in the thinner air, and he was buoyed upward by sheer euphoria.

"If the Sloped Lakes were real, then what about..." Six said.

Geoff waited for him to finish, and gestured impatiently when he didn't.

"...what about Gaixee Marius?"

"No," Geoff said. "That was just kid's talk."

"So were the Sloped Lakes."

The sun began to set as they entered another cloud bank. The trees began to thin, and ground cover was sparse, a layer of pine needles over chalk-white rock, with mineral residue from the quartz tumblers beginning to accumulate like snow. Ahead were lights. Finally the slope crested and plateaued, and the lights, when they reached them, resolved into a single large building, long and slender as a race horse, three stories high and with balconies on the upper floors, an Art Nouveau masterpiece straight out of 1920s Switzerland. Overgrown topiary that faintly retained the shape of giraffes and hippos lined a gravel driveway to the main entrance, above which a sign in lights read "Grand Hotel Teilchenbeschleuniger."

"Hotel...Teil...Teilchen....bes..." Six stammered, trying to sound it out, before giving up.

The mineral snow around the front entrance was several inches thick. A squirrel darted away at Geoff's approach. Inside, a thin layer of the mineral snow covered the foyer and was liberally pockmarked by footprints. The lobby was grand and expansive, with multiple high-backed chairs and sofas and elaborate drinks carts.

"Is anybody here?" Geoff called. His voice echoed. The dog sniffed at a table. Geoff called again, and they waited, but nobody responded. Geoff walked toward a curving staircase that ascended to darkness.

"Don't go up there," Six said.

"Just a quick look," Geoff said. "You can wait here if you like."

***

The long miles show. Salt covers him to the waist, glinting in moonlight as he sits with his head resting on his knees, the closest he comes to sleep. His hands and face are red with tiny wounds, the scars of sawgrass and palmetto shrubs and insect bites. He no longer carries the bulk of a weightlifter. He is still strong, but lean and wiry. His face shows more lines. He has come a long, hard way, in a short time. He is weary, but the night is dark and quiet and cool, and walking is as easy as gliding a finger across a dull blade. He leaves the salt pans and enters a forested slope and he begins to climb.

***

The top floor was elaborately decorated, with a plush red carpet hallway, oak-paneled walls with intricate carved details, and brass sconce lighting directed downward. The room doors were all closed apart from one at the far end of the hall, from which he heard soft music playing. A cold breeze blew across his face as he approached the open door and found a luxury suite with French doors opened to a balcony. Gauzy white curtains billowed inward with the breeze. Beyond them, on the balcony, he saw there were two people reclining in loungers, wrapped in thick blankets against what he now realized was true winter cold. He stepped inside the room. Before he could say anything, one of the people on the balcony turned and saw him.

"You there," a voice said from under the blankets. "Come out here."

The figures didn't move and nobody appeared to be armed, but he still felt a tremor of threat. He looked over his shoulder for Six and the dog, but he was still alone.

He walked outside, his breath billowing in front of his face. He didn't understand how or why it had become so cold. The mineral residue covering the landscape in every direction looked like real snow. What appeared to be icicles hung from the edge of the roof above them.

"We watched you," the voice said, raising a blanket-shrouded arm to point down the slope, indicating the path by which they'd arrived. "Are you here to take the cure?"

He took a cautious pair of steps toward the balcony railing so he could face them. They were completely wrapped in heavy blankets, with a conical opening at the face that was too small and dark to reveal anything about whomever was inside.

"We had a mission," he said.

"To come here?"

"To find a place," he said. "But I don't think this is it."

"Why not?"

He looked at them, their conical hidden faces turned toward him, the air even colder now.

"Because I don't think any of this is real."

"What's real and what's not real. We were just having that debate for the millionth time. My name is Cavallo. That's Lukac. Do not listen to anything Lukac says. Lukac is a liar and a fanatic."

"I'm only one of those, and proud of it," Lukac replied.

"What is this place?" Geoff asked.

"This is where we take the cure."

"The cure for what?"

"For modern ailments of the lung," Cavallo said.

"How long have you been here?"

"Oh, well, since before the war, at least," Lukac said. "Time is different for us. You probably feel like you just arrived here, correct? But we saw you arrive weeks ago. Or am I wrong again?" Lukac asked, turning to Cavallo.

"It was precisely three weeks."

Geoff had a flash behind his eyes, a rapid series of images: arriving with Six, exploring the building, sleeping in comfortable beds, eating food stocks from a massive kitchen, the dog running freely through the halls. No specific memories or feelings were attached to any of these images; they were just pictures. Had it actually been three weeks?

There was another flash of memory. A figure that had followed them, one he hadn't seen of late, the shark man, now somewhere in the building with them.

And another: a figure that was still coming, yet to arrive, but close.

"However long it's been, you are welcome here," Cavallo said. "Make yourself comfortable. There will be time later for whatever you're searching for."

"But there's not time. If this isn't the right place, I have to find the right place. That's the only way I can go home."

Cavallo leaned forward and plucked one of the hanging icicles from the roof edge. "Hand me your water glass, Lukac," Cavallo said.

"I'm drinking that."

"Hand it over. You can get another easily enough."

The pitch and timber of their voices changed with almost every word, Geoff noticed, like voices recorded on tape and played back at varying speeds. At first he thought Cavallo to be a woman and Lukac a man, but he changed his mind and then changed it back again. He had a sense that it didn't matter anyway.

Lukac handed Cavallo the water glass, and Cavallo dropped the icicle into it.

"In the time this takes to melt, you'll have found what you've been looking for. Then it's only a matter of you deciding."

"Deciding what?"

"Deciding whether to stay with us or not."

"Why would I want to stay here?" Geoff asked.

"Give it a chance," Cavallo replied. "You've only been here three weeks."

***

Some of the rooms at the hotel changed every time Geoff walked by them. The carpet might be green one time he passed, then red the next, then entirely gone. Occasionally he saw hotel staff like bellhops and concierges in formal uniforms, and vacationing guests, but they were slightly translucent and took no notice of him.

"Ah yes," Cavallo said, when he mentioned this to him. "Some people have been here even longer than we have. Maybe they've gone away, but something of them lingers. Almost like a film strip superimposed over our reality."

"That's not what it is," Lukac said. "It's just ghosts."

"Ghosts!" Cavallo repeated, in a mocking tone.

"Yes, ghosts. You tell me," Lukac said, turning to Geoff. "Which do you think is more plausible? This hotel somehow being a portal to other times, other dimensions? Or simple ghosts, which have been a part of the culture and experience of every human civilization since the dawn of time?"

"It doesn't matter what is more plausible," Cavallo said, before Geoff could answer. "It only matters what is true."

"This is where we differ, you see," Lukac said to Geoff. "Cavallo has fanciful beliefs about the true nature of reality. He believes our senses limit our experience of reality to the rational. He believes that if we had more or better sensory perception, like bats or dolphins—"

"Oh, let's not start all that again," Cavallo said. "It's thunderously boring."

"This must be very tedious for you," Lukac said to Geoff. "But we don't get many people here. You're the first since—how long has it been?"

"Years. Many years."

"You've been here that long? Couldn't you just leave?" Geoff asked.

"Who wants to leave? Not I," Cavallo said. "It's wonderful here."

"Mostly," Lukac said.

"Yes," Cavallo conceded. "Mostly."

"What do you do here?"

"Mostly we take the cure," Cavallo said. "We lie out here wrapped up against the cold, letting the temperatures and the sun fight infection or fungal growth or parasites, whatever the case may be."

"Do you have medication?"

"There is no need. This air and sun is the cure."

"So what else—"

"We read books," Lukac said. "I'm partial to plays, you see. Sometimes we read the parts together."

"Chekhov, mostly," Cavallo said. "Ibsen. Beckett. Molière."

"Whatever we find in the library."

"Are you just going to stay here forever? Don't you have homes and families?"

Cavallo and Lukac turned their conical shrouded heads toward each other. "My dear lad," Cavallo said, reaching up with both hands to remove his shroud.

"Don't," Lukac said. "Not now."

Cavallo lowered his hands. "As you wish."

Geoff was fascinated by the two of them and their strange, idyllic life here, but he was troubled by the apparent increase in his mind's ability to construct newer and more elaborate fever dreams and fantasy worlds. None of this is real. It's not real, he told himself. This is an abandoned hotel. Nobody is here. If this once was, or still was, Depot 655, or any kind of Dirt Tiger installation, he had to find evidence of it.

He left them, went downstairs, and found Six playing with the dog in the lobby.

"Have you seen enough?" Six asked. "Is this the place?"

"How long have we been here?"

"I don't know, fifteen minutes maybe?" He picked up a stick he'd brought from outside and threw it, and the dog ran through the dusting of mineral snow after it.

***

He woke to a single sustaining note, as if from a bagpipe, coming from somewhere upstairs, where Cavallo and Lukac lived. From the next room, he heard the dog softly coo in response. The note held, with tiny quavers and fluctuations, through the cold night, the dog cooing intermittently, until it faded with sunrise.

"Another one of you came last night," Cavallo told him when he went upstairs.

"Another Free Stater?" he asked, confused.

"I don't know what that is," Cavallo said. "I just know it was someone who looked vaguely like you. But wasn't you."

"You don't know what The Free State is?"

"Can't say I do, although at a guess, it sounds like a failed utopian commune."

"No, it's...you said someone else came here? I should go see."

He went down to the lobby, where Six, evidently living in a different timeline, was still throwing a stick for the dog. "What are you looking for now?" he asked, but Geoff just kept walking. Nobody was in the den or the restaurant, and there was no evidence of the echoes of past guests or employees. He opened the door to what he thought was the old exercise room, full of vintage machines and equipment like vibrating belts and kettlebells, and instead found a short, dark hallway leading to another door. He put his hand on the door and paused. It felt cold and damp. He pushed it and it opened to the library.

Standing in the center of the room was a tall man Geoff had never seen before.

They looked at each other for a long time without speaking. Geoff realized for the first time that he didn't have his weapon, and moreover, could not recall when last he'd even seen it. He'd stopped carrying it when they got to the hotel, however long that had been, although he didn't recall it being a conscious decision. From behind him, he could hear Six cheering on the dog.

It took a moment, but Geoff slowly realized the tall man was not actually staring at him, but at a spot behind him on the bookshelves. He walked past him, close enough to touch, and plucked a book from the shelf. He turned the pages, inspected the back cover, then replaced it.

"Six," he called over his shoulder. "Come here."

The tall man inspected another book. Geoff heard Six come up from behind him.

"Are we sleeping here tonight?" Six asked.

Geoff waited to see if Six saw the man. "How long have we been here?" he asked.

"Why do you keep asking me that? About thirty minutes now."

"Yes," Geoff said. "We're sleeping here tonight."

Six ran back to the lobby, calling to the dog. The tall man sat with a book in an easy chair. Geoff backed out out of the library and closed the door.

***

Geoff found Cavallo and Lukac on their balcony. "I saw him," he said. "He was in the library."

"Did this person say what he's doing here?" Cavallo asked.

"He couldn't see me."

"Ah yes. That may change if you encounter him elsewhere on the property."

"You still haven't told us what *you're* doing here," Lukac said.

"Not that you aren't welcome," Cavallo hastened to add.

"We had a mission," Geoff said. "We were looking for a place called Depot 655. There was some kind of radio broadcast coming from it. We were supposed to shut it down."

"Why, was it offensive?" Lukac asked. "Was it jazz?"

"What? No, it was Dirt Tiger propaganda. Or, that's what they told us it was."

"I suppose I should ask who the Dirt Tigers are. But I'm not going to," Cavallo said, holding up a hand to cut Geoff off.

Cavallo and Lukac lay bundled against the cold. The sun splintered into brilliant chromoflares of colored light as it sifted through the gauze of the quartz tumbler layers that permanently enshrouded the hotel, but the chromoflares brought no warmth. Cavallo reached up to adjust the conical swaddling of blankets which covered their face. It occurred to Geoff he had still not seen either of their faces, but at this point it seemed impolite to mention it.

***

After two of his days, he went back to the library. Six was still in the lobby with the dog, though now they were both napping on an overstuffed sofa. The library was empty, but the table next to the easy chair had three books on it. He picked them up and haphazardly shelved them, then left the room. He went back inside a minute later and two different books were now on the table, and the tall man stood inspecting the shelves with his back to him. Geoff picked up the two books and shelved them. He went outside again, waited, then went back in. This time the library was empty and there were no books on the table. But in their place was a small, handwritten note. He picked it up. It read, "Stop."

***

There was the flight near a storm above the Florida Keys where the entire plane became engulfed in St. Elmo's Fire, the propeller tips glowing blue, with tiny fractals of electricity spreading across the airframe. There was the derelict power plant near Novomoskov, where residual energy caused dust to ripple and dance across empty floors. There was the injured deer he found deep in a Virginia forest that followed him for days but resisted all his efforts to treat its wound. But never has there been anything like this hotel. He still has a job to do and knows how to maintain his focus in the face of strangeness and phenomena. He is not surprised or alarmed by the changing rooms or ephemeral shapes and figures moving through the halls and lobby; he thinks them a trick of his own mind, wracked now with fatigue and sleep deprivation. The only thing that troubles him is the cold. It is everywhere and he can't seem to warm himself, not even wrapped in blankets in an oak-walled room. The tall man has never liked the cold.

The hotel is cold and full of phenomena but he persists with the strangeness because he knows without question he is in the right place. What he has been looking for is here. He just has to find it.

***

Dear Geoff,

The world it seems is getting back to normal. The solar storm has ended and already new satellites are being launched. Soon we will all be connected once more. I have been reading about the mass desertions and the 'Opt Out' which I take it has been something of a disaster. I hope for your sake you haven't been caught up in it, but equally I hope you are ready for a new chapter in your life. There are general strikes and demonstrations being planned, and the rumor is the government is going to make good on the promises they made you. Full university tuition, loan forgiveness for those already with degrees. It could be perfect for you, if you're ready.

I too am ready to get back to normal. I finally had the talk with my father. He took it well. He understands. But to my surprise, I've found I don't want to entirely give up farm life. So I'll continue to commute, only it'll be the city during the week, and the farm for weekends.

This feels like either the end of something or the start of something, or I guess both. I hope you are safe, and finding your way, but mostly I hope you are on your way home. It feels like it's time for this entire misguided operation to end. I can't say why, but I hope you feel the same way.

Stay safe.
I love you.
Elena

***

The hotel seemed larger every time Geoff set out to explore it. The ends of hallways of the top two floors seemed to recede away from him as he walked, and they featured turns and angles not suggested by the simple rectangular exterior. Some doors were locked, and some he could open. The rooms were usually empty and tidy. Some of them were dark and elaborately decorated, others modern and spare. Still others were outfitted as medical treatment rooms, with padded tables and full-scale model skeletons. At a bend in a third-floor hallway, he found a small theater, preserved without a hint of dust or decay. Four rows of overstuffed reclining theater seats arced in front of a screen framed by heavy burgundy curtains. A red 'exit' sign glowed on the wall, but he couldn't see an exit. The projector, behind a glass pane at the top of the wall opposite the screen, blinked to life, and a Pathé News reel began, narrating the events of a horse race in England sometime in the 1930s. A brass flagpole on the stage fell over with a clang, startling him. He sat in one of the theater seats and watched the news reel until it ended with a clattering sound, as if the film strip ran out of the spool. He got up to leave, but first walked up onto the stage. He ran his fingers down the cool felt surface of the burgundy curtains, then noticed, tucked behind them, a small door.

He opened the door to a small, brightly lit room, full of modern furniture and electronic equipment. A middle-aged woman sat inside a plexiglas enclosure, wearing bulky headphones. She read from a script in her left hand: "This is Sister Susie with Dirt Tiger Radio. To all the Free State volunteers who threw down their arms and turned their backs on this government's lies, we say welcome back to the world. Welcome back to your lives. Let's try to build something better, together. Let's do it the right way. No more lies, no more propaganda. This government would have dragged this conflict out forever, lying to you the entire time, breaking promises. We have never been enemies. We have always had a common enemy. This is Sister Susie, coming to you from the mountains of The Big West, and this is Dirt Tiger Radio."

Her eyes flicked up directly at him, but there was no recognition or acknowledgment of his presence. It was already familiar here, this understanding that the person in front of you isn't really there, or you aren't, not at the same time, at least. He watched her for a few minutes as she fiddled with the recording equipment, made herself a cup of tea, and sat down to type at a laptop. Then he backed out the door and into the theater, trying to commit the location to memory.

***

"I saw her," he said to Cavallo. "The woman I came here to see."

"The radio broadcaster?"

"Yes. She's here. This really is Depot 655."

"It's the Grand Hotel Teilchenbeschleuniger. As strange as it is, I don't think it can be two different things."

"I think it's the hotel in your time. In my time, it's abandoned and being used as an outpost and communication center by these people, the Dirt Tigers."

"But you and I, and Lukac here, are all here together. In our time."

"I haven't figured that out yet," Geoff admitted. "Maybe it's just this part of the hotel, or maybe I'm just imagining you. I have malaria, or at least I did, when I got here."

"You've taken the cure," Lukac said. "The air here has curative properties. That's why people from all over the world come here. You've seen them."

"What are you going to do about this woman?" Cavallo said. "The radio broadcast?"

"I think I have a bigger problem."

"The man in the library," Cavallo said.

"Yeah. I've seen his type. Military advisors, they were called, but really they're mercenaries. I think he's here for the same reason I came here. But I think he means to follow through with it."

"Whereas you do not?"

"I don't think it was ever really about that," Geoff said.

"It was more the journey," Lukac said.

"Maybe the journey changed him," Cavallo said.

"People don't change," Lukac said. "Not like that. Not that fast."

"You are determined to see people in the worst possible light."

"People just are who they are."

"Well," Geoff said, hoping to remind them he was standing right there. "The question now is, what do I do about it? I mean if he's here to actually kill that woman."

"That's an ethical question," Cavallo said.

"It's a moral question," Lukac said.

"It's about right and wrong, not his own personal, subjective standards," Cavallo said. "Killing is wrong, so it's an ethical question."

"But the question isn't 'Is killing wrong' but 'is one obligated to put oneself in danger to prevent a killing?' That's why it's a moral question. It's up to—do I even know your name?"

"His name is Geoff," Cavallo said.

"It's up to Geoff to decide what his obligations are."

They turned their blanket-covered heads toward him. He looked out across the faux winter landscape, the towering pines covered in white, treeless mountaintops rising above them, brilliant swords of chromoflares sparkling through the quartz tumbler layer.

"At this point," he admitted, "I don't think I'd feel right about just leaving."

Cavallo and Lukac turned back away from him, and all three looked across the cold landscape. A large black bird landed on the railing of the balcony with a tremendous fluttering of wings, and walked a few steps further away from them before settling down in the mineral snow. Every few minutes, it emitted an abidingly human sigh. It sat with them and they all watched the sun fall behind the mountains, dimming and then extinguishing the chromoflares, until the skies darkened and a steady wind began to lean the trees.

***

Come for the air. Cold and clean, far from city pollutants and noxious vapors, far above the fetid jungle rot, it's air that brushes up against the heavens. Gas exchange in the lungs is optimized, while appetite and immune system function are boosted, and blood flow increases. In addition to our special high-altitude air, the mountain sun is unlike anything you've ever experienced. Heliotherapy is the most exciting medical development of the twentieth century. Irradiating the skin renews cells and diminishes the ability of skin and bone tuberculosis to flourish. Come to Calem, with European luxury and tropical sunshine year-round, loyal subjects of His Majesty George V and governed locally by Lord Malisse, Viceroy of Calem.

Here at The Grand Hotel Teilchenbeschleuniger, we offer a return to the real you, before illness. Electric light, low-pressure steam heat, and private balconies or terraces for every room are standard, as are six full, rich meals per day to reinvigorate the blood. Entertainment and relaxation are guaranteed, with a variety of music salons, a full theater, reading rooms, and an art gallery. Doctor visits and treatments are scheduled at long intervals to allow for hours of cure time in the outdoor air. And speaking of doctors, we've imported, at great expense, some of the finest doctors and surgeons from Switzerland, so you'll receive the highest standard of care in the world.

Come to The Grand Hotel Teilchenbeschleuniger today. Feel better tomorrow.

–ad for The Grand Hotel Teilchenbeschleuniger in 'The Spectator' Magazine, London, 1922.

***

It is easy to find what you are looking for. The tall man has always known this. What you are looking for is always at the center, and the center is always the spot that everything else seems to be moving away from. He has quickly made sense of this place, with its seemingly interchangeable rooms and angled hallways and rotating suites and dens. It is all just a process of cell renewal, old rooms and floors and walls moving out and away from the center, replaced by new ones that seem to simply pop into existence. The Hotel Teilchenbeschleuniger is a living organism. Through a labyrinth of curved hallways and stairs that rise and fall simultaneously, he finds a door that is cold and damp to the touch, and when he opens and enters it, he is standing in an enormous natatorium.

The room is four stories high, the upper floors lined with balconies which overlook the pool. It is like a grand ballroom with a pool, with magnificent glass chandeliers hanging from chains, and a single skylight window nearly the size of the pool. The pool water is a rich, deep blue, which shifts to green and even copper as he walks around and looks at it from different angles. Through the skylight, he sees into the night sky. Some kind of celestial event is taking place. An extremely bright spot in the night sky is radiating waves of blue light outward, pushing stars and entire galaxies along in its wake. Whatever it is, it is happening too far away for his concern.

He knows the radio broadcaster is here; he has already seen her. He can finish his mission at his leisure. But something suggests to him he has found the beating heart of this living museum. He stoops down by the pool and drags his fingers across the flesh of the blue-green water. It is warm, and his fingers, when he withdraws them, retain a faint sparkle of color.

He looks up again at the celestial event through the skylight. The spreading blue ring of light, like clouds illuminated from within, has drawn closer. Now he looks down at his hands, and he sees they are the soft and unlined hands of a child.

***

In the lobby, Geoff found Six and the dog still at play. Six had stopped questioning the Big West version of reality when he saw the Sloped Lakes, so he accepted Geoff's story that they had been there for weeks, even though for both him and the dog, little more than an hour had passed.

"I saw her," Geoff said. Six knew who he meant.

"What's she like?"

"I don't know. She didn't see me. But this is the place."

"Okay. What are you going to do?"

"There's someone else here," Geoff said. "Reaper, I think. I think he has the same mission as us."

"Oh, good. Let him handle it, then."

"You want her dead?"

"What? No. You think he's here to kill her?"

"Have you forgotten what they're like? I don't think he's here to ask her nicely to stop."

In the early days, they'd had training from WHINSEC operatives—they called them "Reapers" because of their apparent thirst for combat—from the United States. WHINSEC stood for Western Hemisphere Institute for Security Cooperation, an American initiative formerly known as the School of the Americas. Sometimes the operatives accompanied them in the field, where they forced confrontation with the Dirt Tigers in situations Free State units would have easily avoided. The operatives were intense and humorless, usually ex-CIA or Special Forces. Eventually they stopped seeing anyone from WHINSEC. The rumor was the Americans had grown frustrated with the unspoken ceasefire and had withdrawn, but small bands or even individuals had been thought to have continued conducting guerrilla campaigns in the countryside on their own.

"Well, shit," Six said. "Maybe you could warn her or something?"

"That's the least we can do."

"The least we could do is nothing. We could turn around and leave."

"You're right," Geoff said. "But I saw her. You didn't."

"Look at you," Six said. "Displaying basic human compassion. This place has changed you."

"You joke, but I think it has."

Six absentmindedly tossed the stick to the dog, who slalomed between lobby sofas to retrieve it. "So what are you proposing?" he asked. "We try to take this guy out?"

"That wouldn't end well for us," Geoff said. "But this place is definitely not normal, and I think I'm starting to understand it. There might be a way to use that."

Six threw the stick again. The dog, finally tired, let it thump to the floor, before curling up at Six's feet. Six reached down to scratch its neck.

"It's such a long way home from here," Six said.

"I know."

"I really want to make it home again."

"I do too."

"Okay," Six said. "Just remember that. Whatever you decide to do...just remember that."

***

The airplane dreams had stopped. The headaches and fever, the chills, the marrow-deep nerve pain, all of it was gone. Maybe, as Lukac suggested, he had taken the cure. Maybe things like malaria just don't exist in this place. But he wasn't back to normal, exactly. For one thing, he could not recall eating or drinking anything since he'd been at the hotel, nor had he been hungry or thirsty. He slept, but it was as if by rote. He didn't grow tired in the evening; he just got into bed at the end of the day, and woke the next morning. If he had dreams, he couldn't remember them.

Only one thing seemed to have come with him from the lowlands.

Geoff saw him in profile, the aviators propped atop his head, at the end of one of the hallways. When he reached the spot, the shark man was gone. He saw him several times around the hotel, but the shark man never acknowledged him. Instead, he began seeing him in the lobby, watching Six and the dog from a distance. The dog saw him, too, snarling more than once in his direction. But Six, as yet, did not.

One night he woke to a faint orange glow outside his window. He rolled over and looked outside. It came from down the slope, far below, where they had walked through jungle and across the salt pans and up the slopes of the foothills, finally reaching these glacial heights, cloaked in cloud. Whatever the glow was, though, it came from far away, it unnerved him, and for the first time at the hotel, he had difficulty sleeping.

All things converging, he'd once been told. Unimaginable forces coming together in one place, for one end. A destiny awaiting each of them, right here.

***

The tall man is intoxicated by the water of the pool, the way microcurrents and underwater thermals twist and mix the sparkling green and blue colors together. It smells of too much chlorine, like the community pool of his childhood, where a sign warned that urinating in the pool was grounds for banishment for the entire summer. There was a rumor they'd put something in the water that would change color if you peed. Nobody dared, not even the bravest or most craving of attention. The tall man has had a lot of memories since coming to the hotel, things he had thought forgotten. There are triggers around every corner, but they are most abiding here, in the natatorium, and the smell of chlorine is the strongest of these triggers. He can't remember the exact year—sometime in the mid-1980s, he thinks—and he can't remember the names of the songs or the bands and the TV shows. He can't remember who he was back then. The decades of his life in the interim, the choices he has made, the training and indoctrination and the missions so often culminating in death, all of it has made such memories trivial, and rendered the details vague. But what he now remembers is the feeling. What it was like before he was feared. What it was like to neither chase nor be chased. He finds it intoxicating, and so he stays at the pool.

He knows there are others here beside himself and the woman. What their purpose is, he doesn't know or care.

He dips his fingers into the water again, and now it's a new-forgotten memory, stirred up like sediment from the bottom of the pool, and the feelings which accompany it are like sunlight falling through trees.

***

Geoff found his way back to the theater and the recording studio at the back. Sister Susie wasn't broadcasting this time but was in the booth, leaning over a laptop. He tried stepping directly in front of her, outside the glass, and waving his arms, but she didn't respond. He reached forward tentatively and rapped on the glass with his knuckles. This time he thought he saw her react, so he knocked again.

"I see you," she said, not looking up. "What do you want?"

"You saw me this whole time? Why didn't—"

"People come in and out of this place every day," she said. "Some I see, some I don't. I have things to do."

"I have to tell you something."

She looked up at him above her glasses. "Are you going to make me ask you what it is?"

"There's someone here to kill you."

"Okay," she said.

"You don't sound worried."

She looked back down at her laptop. "It's not hard to find a radio signal. People have come out here before."

"This one is a Reaper. I don't know if you know—"

"I know what a Reaper is."

"So you know it's serious."

She looked up again. "I know what it takes to come out here." She nodded toward the tattered Free State patch on his shoulder. "The rest of you all went home. But you came out here. Just to warn me?"

"No," he admitted. "I think I had the same mission as him. Not the same. Similar."

"But you changed your mind."

"It seems pretty pointless now."

"Well, I'm overcome with gratitude. You've warned me. You can go now."

"What are you going to do?"

"About what?"

"About the Reaper," he said.

Her tone softened. "You're really worried."

"I've seen how Reapers operate."

She drummed her fingers on the tabletop. "He won't find me."

"I found you."

"But he won't. He'll find something else more interesting than me."

"How can you be sure?"

"I'm not," she admitted. "But I've been here longer than you."

***

The orange glow in his window grew brighter through the night. Even in the steel-bright sunrise of morning, he could see it, tinting the quartz tumbler layer like a tangerine frosting. The glow nagged at him and reminded him of something from his fever hallucinations—so long ago now, it seemed—but he couldn't place it.

He went back to the theater but found the old gymnasium in its place. He watched a young woman strap herself into an exercise belt machine, while another performed a tumbling routine to polite applause from a dozen onlookers. He followed an unfamiliar hallway with elaborate wall sconces, floral wallpaper, and plush green carpeting. An aristocratic dandy in a paisley overcoat emerged from one of the rooms and surprised him by not only seeing him, but addressing him.

"Well!" the dandy said. "And you must be the fitter and turner, yes? Sent by the concierge? It's quite alright. I fixed it myself."

"Fixed what?" Geoff asked.

"The washbasin. I have turned a wrench before, you know, though you might not guess it to look at me. Oh no," he said, gesturing toward Geoff. "This won't do at all. Do you mind?" He reached out and straightened Geoff's collar and patted down the rumpled front of his shirt. "They ought to dress you better."

He nodded politely at Geoff and walked away down the hallway.

Eventually, the hallway ended at a set of stairs. The stairs narrowed as Geoff ascended. Handwriting covered the walls, a series of numbers Geoff recognized as dates, many of which had not yet happened.

The stairs spilled him into a large, bright room, a natatorium with an enormous glass skylight. In an Olympic-sized swimming pool in the center of the room, a middle-aged couple he realized was his parents treaded water. He was not surprised to see them here. Geoff took a step closer to the pool. The water was green with algae growth, but clear enough that he could see the dark silhouette of an enormous crocodile at the bottom of the deep end. He pointed in alarm.

"Don't worry," his father said. "That's just Salty."

"He can't hurt us," his mother said, smiling.

It was nighttime outside. Through the glass walls beaded with condensation, oversized stars and planets revolved through the night sky. Every time he focused on a star or comet or any other celestial body, it flared so brightly it hurt his eyes, and then burned away to darkness. He swept his eyes across the starry panorama and extinguished entire archipelagos of galaxies.

"Oh, honey," his mother said, still treading water. "Don't look up there. You're killing everybody."

The crocodile at the bottom of the pool began to stir.

"He's coming," his father said, smiling.

The crocodile breached the surface, its body covered in jewels.

"What are you two doing here?" Geoff asked them.

"Is this a trick question?" his father asked with a laugh. "We're swimming."

"It's good for the constitution," his mother said. "Doctor Charlton says so."

"Doctor Charlton died when I was a boy."

"We just saw him yesterday, honey. That's why we're swimming."

He watched them treading water languidly. He was overcome with grief and longing and the desire to jump in the pool and hold them both. But it's not really them, he reminded himself.

"Can we go back home?" he asked. "Together?"

"Oh, honey, I'm so sorry," his mother said. "We have to stay here."

The crocodile began to heave its bulk out of the pool, swinging its enormous head toward him.

"Then I want to stay too."

"No," his mother said. "You have to go live your life."

"But I want to stay with you."

She smiled and his heart broke in a way he didn't think possible. He sank to both knees and covered his face with his hands. He heard the wet sounds of the crocodile dragging itself across the tile floor, and his parents playfully splashing, until they faded to white noise, and when he looked again, he was alone, the pool empty and the water as still and flat as mercury.

***

Now there is a scene playing before him, projected into the vapors rising like a screen from the pool. He is young and strong, at a time of his life when he thought it important to appear brave despite his fear. There was a mission in a desert country—the details of it are long forgotten, or suppressed, but he remembers that mistakes were made and it went badly and some people were killed. He has a prisoner of some kind, a young man his own age, on his knees with his hands bound behind his back, left alone with him. The young man posed no threat, had simply been in the wrong place at the wrong time, and they'd captured him. He remembers that this was an opportunity for mercy. He remembers that he did not take the opportunity.

Now, with a wave of his hand, he can wind back the video reel of the memory, and he can change the outcome. He sees himself unbind the young man's hands, sees him stand, shake the stiffness from his arms, and walk back to his life, away from the soldiers.

No particular feeling comes to him from watching this act of mercy. But he rewinds it again and again, and chooses mercy each time, and wonders, had he made this choice at the time, who he might have become.

***

Geoff had seen her before, of course. Many times, he had spoken with her and even held her. But that was always when in the throes of fever. This time it was different. He was lucid and healthy, and she was standing in front of him, not ephemeral but solid and real. She smiled and held out both hands to him, and he reached out and took them. Her skin felt warm and soft, as it should.

"Hello, sweetheart," she said. "Welcome home. I've waited so long for this."

Behind her was the little house in the center of the bean farm. He could see her father in the distance, bent over a row of flowering shrubs.

"Aren't you happy to be home?"

"I'm...just a little tired."

"Now you can rest. Poor Geoff. How far you've come. Look at you." She flipped open his tattered shirt. "You're skin and bones. I'll make dinner."

Cold water dripped onto his head. He looked up. Condensation from the skylight above the pool. He tried to speak but couldn't.

"I'm not really here," he finally said. "I'm still at the hotel."

"You're forgetting what matters," she said. "We're together again."

He started to object, but she stopped him. "Just tell me how it feels. Hold me, and tell me how it feels."

She pulled him close and they embraced, tentatively at first. He put a hand on the back of her head, felt the silky fineness of her hair. He lowered his face to the back of her neck and breathed deeply of her. She was exactly as he remembered. The months of pain and sickness and hunger, the years of loneliness and regret, his powerful longing, all abated as he breathed her in. What felt like a lifetime of hurt could end if he just stopped fighting and gave in to it.

"You're not really Elena," he said softly.

She pulled back from him. "Do I feel like Elena?" She nodded in assertion for him. "So what else matters?"

"If you're Elena, then let's go home together."

Another cold drop of water landed on his head. He wiped it away.

"We're already home," she said.

"But—"

"Maybe she didn't wait for you," she said. "Have you thought of that? Maybe you go all the way back there just to find that out."

He stepped back to look at her. Her green eyes flashed with emotion. As they always did.

"Stay," she said. "Stay here with me."

He looked around at the little house in the center of the fields, dry now in the months following summer. Little whirlwinds of dust bordered the edges of his vision. A drop of water fell into the dust with a "paff" sound. He looked up through the skylights at the arced tail of a comet, blown by solar winds like the feathers of a trogon.

She pulled him close again and whispered. "Stay with me. Why take the chance? She might be gone forever. You know it's possible."

He felt the ocean of his heart swell and didn't know if he could take any more. He buried his face again in the back of her neck and breathed as deeply as someone about to slip under icy waters, and ready to do it.

***

The visions and memories have started to change the tall man. He can feel it. He is dimly aware of his mission, his duty, but he is more keenly aware than ever that all he has ever lived for is duty.

"I am guilty of dereliction of my soul," he says to himself. The words echo faintly round the natatorium.

Another memory plays in the pool vapors. A skating rink he went to as a boy. Colored lights, a mirror ball hanging from the ceiling, and that song. That song that always played at the skating rink. He turns up the volume of the memory to hear it. "Philadelphia Freedom." He loved that song. His friend Kevin made fun of him when he said that once, but then later admitted he loved it, too.

The marvel of these memories is how much like everyone else he once was.

The memory suddenly flickers, freezes, then stops.

Across the pool, on the other side of the natatorium, he sees a shape manifest through the mist. It's him. Their circles have overlapped more than once here, but not yet fully.

His shape flickers again, fades, and then snaps into sharp relief. He is there, standing across the pool, looking directly at him.

They stand and look at each other for some time before the tall man finally speaks.

"What do you see here?" he asks the man.

The man doesn't answer right away. When he does, his voice is at a remove, as if it's coming from very far away or from a very long time ago, and it doesn't seem to quite sync up to his mouth's movements.

"I see my dead parents," he answers.

He nods, as if the answer doesn't surprise him. "Anything else?"

"I'm not sure I should say more. You're a Reaper."

He winces. "That's not a name I would call myself."

"It's what we call you. You don't have a say in it."

"What do they call you?" he asks the man.

"Geoff."

"What are you doing here?"

"Again," Geoff says, "I'm not sure I should say."

"I watched you," the tall man says. "In the bush. I watched all of you sleeping. Nobody on watch. That's when I knew I was going to have to come here. I didn't think there was a chance any of you would bother. But here you are."

"Here I am."

Geoff paced a few steps in either direction.

"It doesn't work with you here," the tall man said.

"Oh? What do *you* see?"

"It's not so much what I see. It's what I feel."

Drops of water fell from the skylight into the pool, where they evaporated right back up and condensed on the cold glass. The comet Geoff had seen earlier was gone. It was an ordinary night sky now, a few stars and clouds, nothing more.

"Well," Geoff said. "I guess we have a problem."

I am so tired of problems, the tall man thinks. So tired. But he doesn't say this.

"Yes," he says instead. "We do."

***

This is Sister Susie with Dirt Tiger Radio. I am still here for you, citizens. This government has tried to silence me so many times, and maybe they will one day. But it's not about me. It's about all of you. If I fall, nothing changes. I am ready for whatever fate has in store for me. I have had the honor of speaking truth to power and representing our movement all these years. I have always known I would be a target. I'm not afraid. This is Sister Susie, speaking to you from the here and now, and this is Dirt Tiger Radio

***

"You look distressed," Cavallo said. "What new development?"

"I saw him again," Geoff said. "In the natatorium. And this time we spoke."

"The natatorium," Cavallo said. "That is not a place I recommend you visit."

"Why not?"

"It's a bit narcotic in there. Something about the vapors from whatever that is in the pool. It's certainly not water. We don't know what it is. You shouldn't trust it."

"It's a strange place," Geoff said. "The entire hotel. Not just the natatorium."

"The secret to this place is the air. The air and those clouds," Cavallo added, raising a shrouded arm to point at the cloaking quartz tumbler layer. "Have you noticed that no matter how heavy the cloud cover, the sunshine comes right through? It's the mineral properties, you see, the chromoflares, rather than moisture, like most clouds."

"Where is Lukac?" Geoff asked. "I only just noticed."

"Oh, his condition is greatly improved. He has resumed his constitutional strolls. I don't see nearly so much of Lukac now."

"How is your condition?"

Cavallo didn't answer right away. "My progress hasn't been as encouraging. But I'm confident this will change soon. Everybody gets better here."

"I hope so," Geoff said. "How long have you been here?"

"Well...I'm not sure I've ever considered that."

"You don't know how long you've been here?"

"I've been here forever. I just don't know how long forever is."

They sat watching the chromoflares tint the mineral snow with color. The great sighing bird landed on the balcony again. Geoff wasn't dressed for the cold and pulled his shirt collar tight against his neck. In the silence, he noticed Cavallo's labored breathing. Geoff stirred uncomfortably in the cold, and began to stand.

"You're going back, aren't you?" Cavallo asked. "To the natatorium."

"Not right this minute."

The bird sighed deeply. They saw Lukac walking in the distance, crossing from the woods to the snow-covered front lawn. The chromoflares began to darken, the most reliable indicator night was coming.

"I've been here forever," Cavallo said again.

***

The tall man finds the theater and the studio at the back easily enough, and Sister Susie in her recording booth. She is broadcasting live. He can hear what she says, but the words have no meaning to him. His entire professional life has been filled with sloganeering and propaganda, and it no longer matters to him from which perspective they come. He has long distrusted the people who employ him. He still has embers of the beliefs that once propelled him, but he has become something worse than a mercenary. He doesn't know what it is; he only knows it's worse.

He wonders now if it's too late.

She finishes her broadcast and looks up at him, takes off her headphones, sits at her desk, and flips open her laptop. Then she slides her chair over a bit so she can turn her back squarely to him. She pauses, fingers hovering just above the keys, like she's waiting for something.

It *probably* is too late, he thinks. But maybe it isn't.

She waits another beat, and then she begins to type.

***

Enough time passed that Six and the dog moved into a room. He spends afternoons on the balcony with Cavallo and Lukac, bathing in chromoflares which blush his skin rainbow hues as they take the cure. He listens as they recite plays, always while reclining but still with commitment and zeal. They do Strindberg and Turgenov and "Cromwell" by Hugo, which they read in French. In the afternoons—he'd learned the tall man was usually there in the mornings—he goes to the natatorium to find "Elena" and walk with her through the snowy grounds outside. She is uncannily like Elena, though there are times he can tell she is just an aggregate of his memories of her. Everything she says is something she has said to him before, repeated verbatim. She often recites her emails to him from months ago as if she is telling him the story for the first time. He takes her back to the natatorium before sunset, where she walks back into the mist and is gone until the next day. This time with her feels close to real, and it sustains him for now. He knows he'll have to leave eventually, but he's not ready.

He makes an effort to avoid the tall man, and the effort appears to be reciprocated. One day, they walked past each other in the hallway outside the theater, and the tall man didn't acknowledge him. But as they passed, Geoff felt a static tremor run along his body. He didn't know what it meant, but he knew it was a bad idea to remain there much longer.

One afternoon, Geoff let the dust whirlwinds at the edge of his vision draw outward and erase the natatorium and replace it with the farm. This time, his perspective was that of an outside eye, watching himself as he went down the rows of shrubs, bending and kneeling, inspecting the leaves, prodding at the soil with a finger. This version of him knew what he was doing, knew how to judge the alkalinity of the soil or the presence of destructive insects. This version of him had never left the farm.

Elena wasn't there, but Snacks was, sometimes chasing after a bird, but usually just ambling alongside him, presenting his head for scratches when offered, his stubby tail a pinwheel blur. Her father worked a few rows over, working faster and more efficiently, but he had to rest more often and for longer, so their progress was about the same. Her father liked this version of him, and would call out things like, "Now this is a good day's work, lad."

A glare came from the road and he shielded his eyes to look. The old Volvo turned into the drive and parked by the house. But that's when he began to lose it, and the whirlwinds started to weaken, and the natatorium began to commandeer his vision. Not now, he thought, although he had known it was going to happen eventually, and then all that was left was the natatorium and the tall man standing across from him.

The tall man, too, finds his experience compromised. There is no memory or vision coupled to what he is feeling. Nobody comes to visit him. He doesn't know how to describe it. He is simply euphoric. There may be snippets of images, but they are unconnected with any events he could remember. But the euphoria is as powerful as a pelagic wave passing above an underwater mountain, one that swells and lifts rather than crashes on the shore. His chest heaves with emotion in ways he has never allowed. It is like hearing birdsong for the first time following a bad storm. He feels many things at once: safe, protected, loved. And then it abruptly ends, and leaves him feeling exhausted, looking across the pool at Geoff.

He tries to speak but can't, not for a long time. There is a hangover from the euphoria, a crushing sadness like a shocking death. He finally composes himself, and speaks.

"Why did you come out here?" he asks.

"We had a mission."

"Yes, I know," the tall man says. "But nobody else cared. Why did you?"

"Why do you care? You only came here for money," Geoff said.

It occurred to Geoff as he said it that it was something Six would've said. He wondered if Six would be proud of him for saying it now.

This is when the migraines and sweating would normally start, the tall man thinks, his central nervous system priming him for violence by releasing a flood of stress hormones into his blood. His fingers would begin to tremble, his vision narrowing and sharpening. But none of that happens now. None of that happens *here*, he thinks.

Some of the euphoria starts to come back to the tall man. Despite this interaction bordering on conflict, he feels his chest fill without taking a breath.

Geoff, on his side of the pool, saw Elena appear on one of the balconies overlooking them. She raised a hand to him. The tall man must have recognized a change in his face.

"What do you see?" he asks.

"I'm coming down," Elena said. The tall man turns to look at her. He can see her.

"Don't," Geoff replied. "Don't."

"She's not real," the tall man says. "It's just this place recycling your memories."

Geoff looked at Elena, now down from the balcony somehow, standing behind and to the right of the tall man, smiling.

"I know," Geoff said.

"Does it feel the same?"

He looked at Elena, still smiling, beginning to walk around the pool to his side. He felt his skin tingle and his breath shorten. "Almost," he said.

Elena's smile widened. "Do you remember the dog—"

"Snacks," Geoff said.

"Yes! He's here with me, you know. On the farm. With my father. It's just you we're missing." She took him by the hand. Again he had the abiding sensation that it could all be over, all the suffering and hunger and illness, and all the walking. He could just stay here. Wherever they were, with whatever she was.

"Why didn't you like it when I ate the lemons?" he asked her.

"What?"

"When I used to eat lemons to show off. You didn't like it, but you never told me why not."

"I remember that."

"But *why* didn't you like it?"

Her face went blank for a moment, then brightened. "Who can remember? That was a long time ago."

He looked at the tall man. "Why haven't you done it yet?"

"The radio woman?"

"Yes."

The tall man crosses his hands in front of him and thinks. "I used to think it was too late for me," he says. "But then I came here."

Elena leans her head against his shoulder. Geoff looks down at her, strokes her hair gently, and eases away from her.

"You can have it," he said to the tall man. "All this. I'm leaving."

The tall man reacts to this by walking around the pool toward him. He stops a few feet away, and they look at each other for a minute, the tall man seemingly trying to make up his mind about something. Finally he sighs and grimaces slightly, and reaches into a pocket. "I won't need this anymore," he says, handing Geoff a small pill bottle.

Geoff took a few steps back. Mist from the pool rose to the skylight. "How do you know she waited for you?" Elena asked again. She was still smiling at him, even as he turned and left.

***

He found Six in a hallway outside his room. "Have you noticed an orange glow outside?" Six asked. Before Geoff could answer, Six said, "It's fire."

***

"We're leaving," Geoff said. "And I just thought you should know about it."

"I'm sure it's fine," Cavallo said.

"Nothing to worry about," Lukac agreed.

"But Six says it looks like a huge fire, and it's moving this way."

"It's just coming home," Cavallo said.

"What does that mean?"

"I can't explain it. But the hotel has it under control. Your concern is touching. We've grown quite fond of you, Geoff. And we'll miss you."

"Yes we will," Lukac said. "You see? You've become the one thing we agree on."

He left them on the balcony, and started toward the hall. He turned to look back at them just as they began to lower the shrouds from their heads, and he hurried away, certain he was not meant to see more.

***

They stood outside on a ridge in the cold, mineral snowdrifts up to their knees, looking down at the slopes below, where a line of fire churned in the forest, a wall of flame twenty feet high in places.

"How far away is it?" Six asked.

"It doesn't matter. It's not real."

"It looks real to me."

A deer surprised them by bounding up from the trees. It stopped in front of them for a moment and looked directly at Geoff, before continuing up and around the hotel.

"I think he thinks it's real," Six said, but Geoff only shook his head.

"It's real," he said. "But it's not fire."

***

Maybe dreams don't come only in sleep, Geoff thought. Maybe when death is near, hovering just behind or all around you, dreams enter your waking world. Maybe to help prepare you to cross over, he thought, or maybe because you're already crossing over, into whatever awaits. He tried to clear his head. He was most definitely awake, standing with Six and the dog, looking at a wall of fire. But something else was also happening.

He was in the air.

In his fever dreams, asleep or awake, or in the liminal spaces between the two, it was always the same plane, a large, commercial airliner. He had never flown on any such plane. He knew what they looked like on the inside only from television shows and movies. But in his real life, he had never left the ground.

In his dreams, he had always flown on the plane alone, or seated next to the shark man. He had sometimes floated freely in the air around the plane, or stood on the ground and watched as it hovered above him. There had always been something about it that he hadn't quite been able to pinpoint, something upsetting, but now, sitting in a window seat, he finally knew what it was: the plane was on fire.

So many powerful forces converging. Internal combustion, jet exhaust, fantastic speed, and fire.

Orange light streamed around him, and his frame cast a shadow on the plane's bulkhead in front of him. He felt heat on the back of his neck. He turned to look out the window.

They were flying alongside a bristling thunderstorm, just off the left wingtip. The black clouds boiled with convection, spitting sabers of lightning in every direction. He looked down. They were flying low. A field hurtled by at fantastic speed. He could see the plane's shadow on the ground with every flash of lightning. There was no sound, not from the lightning, nor the plane's engines. The shark man was next to him, and for once, they weren't alone in the passenger compartment. Scattered through the cabin, sitting motionless with their heads bowed, were figures in street clothes. One of them turned to look at him. Its face was covered in mesh bandage wrappings, permeable enough for him to see that its mouth was open wide, as if howling silently, and he knew he was seeing the ghouls from Six's Village of the Dead.

"I thought it best to be here," the shark man said. "Just in case."

The left wing dipped into cloud. The plane rocked and bumped. Lightning flashed just outside his window. Geoff unfastened his seat belt, stood, and walked forward, toward the cockpit.

"I want to see it for myself," he said.

"That's a good idea," the shark man said. Geoff started again for the cockpit.

***

They started down the slope, Six holding the dog to his chest and protesting, but still following. With every step away from the hotel, Geoff felt twinges of his headache returning, and the stirrings of bone-deep pain, and his skin felt feverish. The fire grew louder; there were pops and snaps and a dull roar, but there was still no heat. Eventually they drew close enough to see that Geoff had been right. Whatever it was, it wasn't real fire, but a kind of hologram or projection, a pyrotechnic light show.

"What do you think it's for?" Six asked.

"Cavallo and Lukac sort of implied the hotel created it."

"Who?"

"Never mind. I'll tell you about them later."

"Can we walk through it?" Six asked.

"We're going to try."

They got close enough to reach out and touch it. Geoff found a long stick and poked it into the projection; it lit up bright orange but didn't burn, and when he pulled it out and touched it, he felt no heat.

"I think we're good," he said.

"You have to go first," Six said. "Sorry. But we're making this decision for the dog, so you have to make sure it's safe first. A dog shouldn't die this way."

Geoff stepped tentatively forward and reached his index finger into the light. It lit up brightly, but he didn't feel anything, so he stepped forward. A low hum filled his head, and the orange light overwhelmed him with luminosity. But he didn't burn.

***

He reached the cockpit—there was nobody to stop him—and opened the door. The panoramic view from the wraparound windows stunned him. They were flying through a clear night sky, stars above them, cities of sparkling light far below. The moon, crescent, lounged in hazy cloud at the horizon. A pair of shooting stars streaked across their path, leaving behind smoke trails illuminated by starlight. They must have flown through the thunderstorm already.

Three pilots turned in their seats to look at him. They wore crisp blue airline pilot suits, with matching blue caps and showy gold epaulets. All three wore medieval plague masks, with long, beak-like noses fashioned of leather, and discs of dark glass covering the eyes. Their hands, protruding from their jacket sleeves, were skeletal.

"Look sharp, lads!" one of the skeletons said from behind his mask.

"A pleasure to serve you, sir," said another.

The three pilots removed their caps, set them on the instrument panel, then raised their right hands and saluted him. A ring on the hand of one of the skeleton pilots slid off his bone finger and landed with a *clink* on the cockpit floor.

"Ah, shit," the pilot said.

The plane flew on through the night. Orange light and heat came from the open cockpit door behind him, but nobody seemed concerned. The pilots held their salute in silence, as the stars rolled overhead and illuminated cities unspooled below, glittering and grand, and in his dream, he knew he was safe.

***

Hi Geoff,

I don't know if you get any news. We got cell phone service back for awhile. My phone went crazy this morning with notifications, but then we lost service again. They think it'll be back for good this week. Right now, it comes and goes.

We have seen each other twice in the last year. I just realized that, looking at some pictures. Twice.

Stay safe. Write some more. I think I'll get them now.
Really, please—stay safe.
Elena

***

Nothing happened in the flame projection. They walked a few hundred yards through it and emerged into normal mountain forest, the mineral snow left behind. They passed the sloped lakes, where fish jumped upward and fell backward and the air grew warmer. Night came as they reached the lowlands and the salt pans. They crossed the pans for hours, the dog trotting alongside them, sometimes running ahead and then waiting, until when Geoff looked back toward the fire, it was just a faint glimmer high in the mountains.

Now in the cradle of night, the fire behind him, there was only the path ahead, the same jungles and fields, small towns and abandoned villages. All that gigantic, brutal land to cross, all over again.

They were on a dirt road leading between fields too dark to distinguish. Stars drifted above. There was no wind or sound at all but for the little dog panting and sometimes whining.

Their rifles were gone, lost in the vortices of whatever the hotel was.

***

They left the eastern highway and tracked through fields and villages, along small roads, toward Margaret Town. There were signs of normalcy. They passed the village of Eagleton, where the people had cleaned up after the hurricanes, piling broken trees and fronds and garbage into mounds and setting them alight. There was too much moisture, so the mounds only smoldered, but it was a start. A man gave them a bottle of water to share and a chicken leg for the dog.

Several times, Geoff had wanted to tell Six everything he'd experienced at the hotel. Cavallo and Lukac, the tall man, Sister Susie, and the general sense of illusion, magic, and wonder. But he didn't know how to start, and he wasn't feeling well enough to try.

Later was a town, Endle Dale. He knew the name. A kid he'd grown up with, Easton McMaster, had moved away to Endle Dale when they were ten.

"This is where we part," Six said, at an intersecting road just outside town. "I have to go south from here. Just another four miles and I'm home. Why don't you come with me? Stay the night. There are buses to Wilshire. You could get where you're going easily enough."

Geoff shook his head. "I'm too close."

Six nodded. "Well," he began.

"No big speeches," Geoff said. He reached out a hand and they shook, and then pulled in for a hug.

"I wish you had seen what I saw at the hotel," Geoff said.

"I saw enough," Six said. "I saw enough to know there's things we can't explain in this world."

"Something like that," Geoff said. He squatted down and scratched the dog on his back. "Give it a name soon, will you?"

"I will."

Six and the dog walked south. He turned once and waved, and then Geoff was alone.

He avoided town center and walked along a dirt road past a few dozen small houses. In front of the last one, two teenage kids were working on a Honda Accord from the 1990s.

"Crank it," said one to the other. "If the distributor turns, we know it's not the ignition."

The other kid turned the key and the engine cranked, but didn't start.

"Shit. Maybe it's the fuel pump."

He could still hear the engine's feeble attempts to turn over as he left town on open road, the sun setting behind him.

Not only had he heard of the next town, Madison, but he had been there before. He had played soccer there two or three times, when he was on his school team. He was close. Just outside Madison, another small stray dog ran up to him. He thought it was Six's at first, but this one was even smaller, and bounded like a puppy. It had no collar or tags, and he made no effort to discourage it following him out of town. A small storm flickered in the night sky ahead of them.

He shivered with fever and ached in the deepest parts of his body. What he suspected was true: the hotel had not cured his malaria; it had only suppressed it.

He remembered the pill bottle the tall man had given him. He pulled it from his pocket. In the faint glow of the last street light on the road out of Madison, he was just able to read the labeling.

Chloroquine.

***

The road was dark, closed in on both sides by the rainforest of the lowlands. He peered into the gloom and saw a familiar figure leaning against a tree, waiting for him.

"You," Geoff said.

The shark man stepped into the road in front of him. They stood facing each other a long time. The dog didn't react to the shark man. The road ahead of them arced over a small hill. From behind it came a hazy light in the night sky: Margaret Town. He was that close.

In the dark, Geoff couldn't see the shark man's face. All he knew was the shark man was back, and he appeared to have been waiting for him.

"You were at the hotel," Geoff finally said.

"I thought perhaps I would be needed. I was mistaken. So for now, our business has concluded. Maybe we'll meet again."

"Not for a long time, I hope," Geoff said.

The shark man tilted his head. Ambient light reflected off his powdered diamond skin.

"There's just no way to know," he said.

A moment later, he was gone in the night. Geoff and the dog walked on. A night wind rustled waxy leaves in the forest.

***

Melaleuca Drive, the little house.

The yard was empty this time. Inside, he found his parents sitting together in their matching chairs, holding hands across the short space that separated them, and singing.

He had never known his parents to sing, except perhaps in church, and even then, he was pretty sure his father only mouthed the words, a distinct lack of enthusiasm for singing being one of the holdovers from their time in the Church of England. But here they were, singing together, beautifully, in the harmony of a chorus of hundreds. It couldn't be them. It couldn't be real.

> O, *mother of the four winds, fill our sails*
> *As we cross those dark seas*
> *Those black waves and wind-feathered gales,*
> *To find peace in your groves and peace in your trees.*
>
> O, *father of the four skies–*

They stopped singing. He moved closer, and sat on the thin oval rug at their feet. His father looked at his mother.

"I've been dead for so long," he said. "And I have so long still to go."

"Oh, me too. Me too," she said.

They smiled serenely. At peace. The room blurred to haze.

He was outside again, but could hear them singing still as he walked up Melaleuca Drive, away from the house. It was daylight, but he could see stars turning in the blue sky, and then it all was gone.

***

The chloroquine had begun to work quickly, loosening the vice grip on his head, easing the pain from his bones as they walked breezily down the muddy road. He was amazed at how the world looked, and felt, and sounded, in the total clarity and lucidity he now had. Each thing he saw was distinct, with sharp edges, a beginning and ending. No more blending, no more miasma of color and sound. Even at the hotel, his illness temporarily suppressed, it hadn't been like this. How long had his brain been muddled by fever, his visions and dreams and nightmares all merging into one approximation of reality, one falsity? He reached a hand down and stroked the small dog, felt each individual coarse hair on its back. The dog squirmed with joy under his touch. He shared the joy. When health returns to a sick body, it brings a flood of energy, the arrogant vigor of youth. They walked together through the night without rest.

"Your name is Seven," Geoff said. "And Elena is going to love you."

Margaret Town was next.

***

Just before sunrise, he slept for an hour in an untended field with Seven curled under his arm. When he woke, the eastern sky was alight, and the stars evaporated in the morning mist. He took another dose of chloroquine. After an hour of walking, they reached Margaret Town. His stomach tightened with nerves. He crossed a neighboring field and then was in the small bean farm, her house in the center. Near it was a white-haired man, bent on one knee, sifting through the small bean shrubs. Seven barked and the man looked at them and stood. Geoff raised a hand. Mr. Telford looked at them for a long time before he spoke.

"You're back," Mr. Telford said.

"Yes, sir."

"On leave?"

He looked toward the house, a hundred yards away, morning sun glinting in its windows. Seven barked again. Geoff reached down and scratched the back of his neck, soothing him. The dog was still uneasy and bristled with energy.

"I think it's over now," he said. "All of it."

The man squatted among the bean shrubs. He nodded at the dog. "What's his name?"

"Seven."

"Elena was going to get a dog, you know," he said. "But she never did."

"There hasn't been trouble here?" Geoff asked. "Deserters?"

"We don't have anything anybody wants."

"That's good," Geoff said.

Mr. Telford began inspecting the shrub leaves of his crops, turning them over and rubbing them between his fingers. "Yes and no," he said. "Yes and no."

The field smelled of fertilizer and fresh growth. Seven dropped to his belly, extending his legs and body across ground not yet warmed by the sun.

"What's that you're doing?" Geoff asked.

Mr. Telford looked up. "You have to watch for beetles and fungus. There's no way to know but to look and feel. The fungus feels like powder."

"What do you do if there is fungus?"

He pushed his hat back and looked at Geoff.

"Are you really interested?"

"I'd like to know."

"Well, there are fungicides. It's not usually a problem here, because I slope the land and keep it drained. But still, you have to check."

A small flock of brown jays burst from a tree and swooped across the fields, calling *pee-ah, pee-ah*. Seven jumped at the sound and barked. Geoff reached down and stroked his matted fur. "Don't be afraid," he said. He would have to wash him soon, and get him a real collar. The dog looked up at him, panting in his excitement.

"She's not home, you know," Mr. Telford said, still turning leaves in his fingers. The sun rose above the trees and flooded the field with the heavy orange blush of morning. Mr. Telford rose to his feet and yawned. He brushed damp soil off his trousers. "She's in the city. She's in the city a lot these days. But she's coming soon. You can wait in the house, if you want."

"I don't mind helping."

"No. Go rest. You look like hell. It would just slow me down anyway, showing you what to do. There's tea and scones on the kitchen table."

Geoff whistled, and Seven, having wandered in the field, sprinted over to him. Seeing Mr. Telford standing, it growled again in alarm.

"I said don't be afraid, little one," Geoff said. "You never have to be afraid again, don't you know?"

From the road he heard a noise, and saw the old Volvo slowing to turn into the driveway, the morning sun reflecting off its windshield. They crossed the field toward the house. Geoff picked up a small stick and lobbed it ahead, and the little dog leapt for it, exultant.

Acknowledgments

I'm grateful to many people for their help in getting *Thunder From a Clear Blue Sky* into the world. This novel started life in very different form while I was a student in the MFA program at New York University. Chuck Wachtel's novel workshop helped steer me in the right direction, and Chuck himself was an immensely kind and generous instructor. All my other instructors in the program deserve thanks as well: Irini Spanidou, Nicholas Christopher, and E.L. Doctorow, whom I was fortunate to have as my thesis advisor.

Two very special publishing professionals saw early promise in my work and have been great friends and champions. I can still count on their support today. Thank you, Deanne Urmy and Erin Edmison.

Huge thanks to Sean Carswell, a fantastic writer who was a crucial beta reader of this manuscript. One of his notes helped move the manuscript away from a real dead end.

Deepest thanks to two writers whose work I love who agreed to blurb requests: Jennifer Wortman and Tobias Carroll. Read their books!

The incredible cover of this novel is thanks to the artistry and vision of Angelo Maneage.

Without Alan Good, this novel and indeed Malarkey Books would not exist. He is a tireless champion of his writers, and we are all extremely fortunate to work with him.

Finally, to the love of my life, my wife Sarah: thank you for the unwavering belief in me. It is worth more than I'll ever be able to express. I hope only to be worthy of it.

Other titles from Malarkey Books

The Life of the Party Is Harder to Find Until You're the Last One Around, Adrian Sobol
Faith, Itoro Bassey
Music Is Over!, Ben Arzate
Toadstones, Eric Williams
It Came from the Swamp, edited by Joey R. Poole
Deliver Thy Pigs, Joey Hedger
Guess What's Different, Susan Triemert
White People on Vacation, Alex Miller
Man in a Cage, Patrick Nevins
Don Bronco's (Working Title) Shell, Donald Ryan
Fearless, Benjamin Warner
Un-ruined, Roger Vaillancourt
Your Favorite Poet, Leigh Chadwick

CPSIA information can be obtained
at www.ICGtesting.com
Printed in the USA
BVHW071829130123
656258BV00004B/870

9 798987 465417